The
Beach House

The
Beach House

by Virginia Coffman

PIATKUS

Copyright © 1970 by Virginia Coffman

First published in Great Britain in 1982
by Judy Piatkus (Publishers) Limited of Loughton, Essex

British Library Cataloguing in Publication Data
Coffman, Virginia
  The beach house.
  I. Title
  813'.54[F]   PS3553.0415

  ISBN 0-86188-135-4

Printed and bound in Great Britain by
Redwood Burn Limited, Trowbridge, Wiltshire

The
Beach House

One

It was late in the day when I started to drive across the island, and I was suddenly afraid I might have to spend the night at Beach House. It didn't help matters that a few minutes out of Honolulu the wind was wet with rain, blowing a gale over the Nuuanu Pali as I started down the grade toward the north coast and the old Thursten home on an isolated beach.

The truth is, Beach House was not a place where I cared to be caught after dark. From the day I, an unknown mainlander named Livia Carter, was hired as Mark Thursten's secretary in place of his sister-in-law, I had never felt comfortable on my infrequent visits to Beach House. This may have been because Mark's wife, Sybil, regarded the place as her own province, and entertained lavishly, with little room for her husband's hired hands. The last time I had visited the house was less than a month after her death, a painful occasion I wasn't likely to forget. I had driven out then to pick up some clothes and books for Mark, while he awaited trial in Honolulu on a charge of murdering his wife.

Now, five months later, as I drove along with the windows down, feeling the brisk salt spray on my face, my thoughts were full of Mark. I hoped things would be better for him, that he could know peace, and eventually even live a normal life again.

I squeezed a little more speed out of my beat-up old green Chevy and chugged along between neat but prickly rows of pineapple, now and then glancing out, as I always did, at the sharp, wet darkness which was the Koolau Range, a kind of spine that caught the storms after they swept across the windward coast where Beach House stood.

The wind was also blowing a gale the afternoon Sybil Thursten died. It was the defense's claim that the wind had blown Mrs. Thursten against the open door of the sun porch-lanai and swept her off the short flight of steps onto the rocks below. That would explain the bloody wound above her temple that actually killed her.

The prosecution contended that Mark and Sybil had quarreled violently just before her death and that he threatened her, a fact repeatedly emphasized by Sybil's mother and sister, and most damaging of all, by Mark's embittered young daughter. For a little while during the trial I had hated those three. But in the end my evidence outweighed theirs, and Mark was free.

In the incomparable way of Hawaiian weather, the late afternoon sun cut through the blue-black clouds in blinding streaks, and my own spirits brightened considerably. I thought that with a little effort I might even be civil to Mark's in-laws, although they had made it pretty impossible on the occasions we had met recently, in the courtroom.

The sun gradually cut away the mist and then the gale, so that when I drove through Haleiwa and another village and turned off the highway along the sandy beach road, the world of the windward coast was suffused in gaudy sunset colors, which made the intervening shadows from the long hibiscus hedges all the deeper. It was the hibiscus, along with the big, spreading beach heliotrope and several ancient *hau* trees, that masked Beach House from the sandy road.

It was surprising and unpleasant to find my fingers stiffening on the wheel as I approached the house. I hadn't thought I could be so cowardly. After all, no ghosts or other signs of Sybil Thursten's shocking death had haunted me five months ago when I came here to pick up Mark's things. But then, five months ago I was so busy I hadn't time to be frightened. Mark's life was threatened, and I was the only person on Oahu who knew he couldn't have murdered his wife at four o'clock. He was in his Honolulu office giving me a birthday charm bracelet at that hour, and I was delighted to say so in court. My evidence was particularly important because I had been one of the few people in the office building and the only one in Mark's office that day, which had been a Saturday. I often came in on Saturdays to catch up on my work.

Nevertheless, though I had only committed a simple act of justice in defending my employer, I knew on the day of his acquittal that I had made enemies of Sybil Thursten's vengeful family, who probably hated me now more than they hated Mark. I suppose it was those two women and Mark's daughter, Bobbie, I was thinking of when I approached Beach House that late afternoon. I had not seen Mrs. Thursten's mother and sister since the day I testified, and then only for a minute or two. I was not acquainted with either of them officially. Sybil Thursten had never introduced me to her mother, Mrs. Jeffrey, or her sister, Carol, so that our acquaintance was a matter of frozen glances and evasive eyes seen across a scandalized, gossiping courtroom. I never mentioned our lack of acquaintance to Mark. He had enough to think about in coping with their enmity.

As I parked in the lean-to under a widespread *hau* tree about a hundred yards from the big wooden house, I realized that I must be the first to arrive after the wholesale departure at the time of the tragedy. I didn't know whether I was relieved or not. I had no desire to encounter the Jeffrey women so soon after the trial, but on the other hand, Beach House was not an appealing home when empty, either.

I got out and walked between gigantic hibiscus bushes whose tangerine and scarlet blooms always seemed unbelievable to me, and stepped out across the rocky beach, remembering too late that the heels of my thonged white sandals might trap me in the sandy stretches. The late sunlight was at my back, casting me in long shadow as I strode across the beach studying the side of the two and a half story house, which was forbidding in its severity. The long windows were Victorian in style and there were no lanais, no porches or verandas on this side. Nor were there Venetian blinds, and it always surprised me to note the old-fashioned flowered chintz portieres and dimity curtains. The place might have been built by a missionary a hundred years ago, and probably was.

I noted that a loose, warped shutter on a window of one of the attic rooms had been caught by the wind off the sea, and was beating a tattoo against the house wall. I would have to go up there and refasten the shutter. I had never been in that part of the house and expected I would find myself knee-deep in trunks, ancient garments, and the debris of a lifetime, but I wanted to spare Mark all I could.

A loud crash somewhere beyond the house, like falling timber, shook me out of my uneasy dreams of returning ghostly wives. I knew there was nothing ghostly about that crash. I hurried across the beach, passed the more prepossessing ocean front of the house with its screened lanais on both floors, and caught my first glimpse of something human on this desolate, windswept shore.

Up on a slight rise above the beach, two young men in blazing *aloha* shirts and swim trunks were building what appeared to be a garage on a foundation of coral with a very shaky roof of timber and palm fronds. The boys had hung their football jackets on a stray *keawe* bush, and I saw that they were both university students, probably picking up a little tuition money after classes. The handsomest boy, with a lean, bright Japanese face, saw me and gave me a big grin. I stepped up over jagged coral rock, careful not to turn my ankle, and said,

"Hi! I'm Mr. Thursten's secretary. Are you fellows going to be doing this very long?"

The Filipino boy exchanged a quick glance with my first greeter, who said, "Sure, Miss Carter. We knew you from your picture in the

Star-Bulletin. You testified for Mr. Thursten. This job? We figure to be through by the weekend if we do a little work each afternoon. Got another garage for us to build? I'm Joe Nakazawa, by the way. And my hardworking buddy is Manuel Bardia."

I laughed. The boy's good humor eased the sense of loneliness and tragedy I had felt about the Beach House.

"I don't suppose you would be interested in helping me take off dust sheets and generally air out the Thursten place when you get through here for the day? It'd be time and a half pay," I reminded them, having myself been induced to work overtime in Los Angeles often enough by the magic phrase "time and a half."

The Filipino student did not even look at the side of the Beach House. He kept his dark-eyed gaze flatly upon the nails he was selecting. "No, thanks, ma'am. Not me. We're leaving soon, anyway."

For the first time Joe Nakazawa's cheerful look faded, though not entirely. He tried to put the best face on his refusal, but it was a refusal all the same. "Sorry, Miss Carter. You want the truth? You wouldn't get me in that mausoleum after dark. Not on your life. Look at it! Just sitting there watching us out of those ugly, wrinkled old eyes."

In spite of myself I turned and looked back

13

over my shoulder at the great, imprisoning side wall of the house, which looked every bit as formidable as the west side except that no shutter was flapping here, and any ghostly inhabitants seemed confined to other parts of the house. The realization that even these healthy fellows were afraid of the place chilled me, and because I shared their feeling, I resented them for calling it to my attention.

"Well, don't make too many more loud noises. You scared me to death."

I climbed down over the coral outcropping and went back across the sand to the seafront of the house. Behind me, Joe Nakazawa called out, "Miss Carter! If you ever need anything like a cab or a phone call, stuff like that—go to my mother's grocery store on the left-hand side as you enter the village. It's called Nakazawa's."

I waved to show there were no hard feelings, and then passed out of their sight in front of the house. I was annoyed to find that with the college boys gone, I was beset by that stupid fear again. I stood on one of the five wooden steps where Sybil Thursten had fallen to her death, and still couldn't see why the woman hadn't cushioned her fall with her arm, since she'd fallen forward. It was such a short drop, and the coral presumably responsible for Sybil's death blow was so unobtrusive—an outcropping of a few square inches—that I could see why there had been so much talk about murder.

I fitted Mark's key into the door of the screened lanai which fronted the first floor in a fashion very like a Midwestern screened porch. Aside from the dust, blown in along with the seasonal gales, the room with its ugly wicker furniture looked as good—or bad—as it ever had. There was an old, surprisingly comfortable couch along the east wall, with a beautifully worked afghan thrown over it, and to one side of the couch, a padded Early American rocking chair. I had seen too many old horror movies to be surprised at the sight of the chair calmly rocking by itself. Obviously the sea breeze explained those creaking movements, but it didn't precisely endear the house to me.

The living room beyond, which was far from light, thanks to the long, curtained windows, occupied at least half the first floor. Sybil Thursten's dinner dances had been held here and in the adjoining dining room. Once when I had been here I had seen the food being prepared in the big, old-fashioned kitchen. Now, with the furniture all shrouded, the room depressed me. I rushed around grabbing off sheets, dropping them in piles on the floor, troubled by my own consciousness of the dead Sybil's influence in this room. Everyone who mentioned her prefaced her name by the word "beautiful," possibly because she laughed a great deal and took nothing seriously. I admired something in that. But I had thought it a mistake in her treatment of her husband. Mark was not a man with an overwhelming sense of humor. Perhaps because of that, his rare smile was doubly wonderful when it appeared. With one last glance at the big living room, I had a sudden, dreadful thought: Was Sybil laughing when she died?

The kitchen, pantries, freezers, Mark's study, and a servant's bed-sitting room completed the ground floor. I left them as they were; most of them would be someone else's department. Then I started up the narrow back staircase to the second floor, where I certainly had my work cut out for me. There were at least six bedrooms, unimaginative and severe for the most part, and all opening off a dark, dingy hall that must have been a severe trial to the gay Sybil. I went through innumerable rooms and baths—some of the latter recent innovations—and took off covering sheets wherever I found them, until I came to the lovely all-white bedroom at the beach front of the house. What I found there shocked me by its difference from the rest of the household furnishings. Aside from the hall door, there were double French doors opening on a private lanai over the bigger one on the floor below. This overlooked the sea, which roared in on the high tide.

The room itself was surprisingly clean and dust-free, with the white bedspread, white curtains, and a woolly-looking white rug all spotless. I had no doubt this was Sybil Thursten's bedroom and I didn't at all like the creeping sensation of her presence somewhere just out of my sight. With her sense of mischief, it would be like her to spring out on her husband's secretary, scaring me to death!

Only, of course, it was Sybil who had been, in a way, scared to death. I circled the room and the dressing room and bathroom behind it, wondering why the dead woman seemed so alive to me here. I discovered the answer belatedly when I found a spilled bottle of Patou's Joy, a perfume I would always associate with Mark's wife.

A loud bang somewhere over my head startled me into a cowardly scream. Then I remembered the loose shutter on that attic room window.

Mark had told me he would have the electricity turned on today, if possible, so it was disappointing when I flipped the wall switch in Mrs. Thursten's room and nothing happened. My hand brushed the milk-glass oil lamp that decorated the chest of drawers near the switch, and for a few seconds, as I felt my way back into the hall, I was not aware of anything unusual. It came to me belatedly that my knuckles were warm from their contact with that milk-glass lamp.

Phantoms hardly need oil lamps, I reminded myself, but the only alternatives were almost equally frightening. Someone else shared Beach House with me tonight, someone uncommonly quiet. I wondered why that silence, and if that silence had anything to do with the condition of Sybil Thursten's bedroom suite which, so clearly, was being used.

It was even possible, of course, that some trespasser was camping here, knowing that none of the family had occupied the house since Mark's arraignment on the charge of murdering his wife. I had intended to call out, but if the trespasser was not a member of the family, I might be in some physical danger ... or even, I added on second thought, if the trespasser *was* a member of the family. I decided to move carefully. I felt my way down the hall to the back of the house, helped by the last orange rays of sunset peering through an end window, and went downstairs, intending to get a flashlight from my car. Passing the kitchen, I noticed a match folder on the Formica shelf beside the two sinks, and searched through the nearest cupboard for a lamp. Almost at once I found an old-fashioned but handy candlestick with a glass hood, a kind of hurricane lamp. There were a surprising number of plain white tallow candles in the silver drawer, and I took one, stuck it into the lamp, and lit it, feeling that I was being none too subtly drawn back into the spiritual era of this lonely house.

I was faintly aware of the banging shutter, probably because one of the kitchen windows was open an inch at the top; so I left the lamp long enough to go outside to the west side of the house and stare up at the attic shutter. This had taken me only a minute or so, but as I looked up at the window, which caught the dying sun in a blaze of reflected fire, I saw that the shutter was motionless. Since the evening breeze still blew, I could only suppose the shutter had been hooked back against the house during the brief interval since I'd heard it banging.

There seemed little doubt that my fellow occupant of Beach House was in the attic at this minute and very likely had heard my entire progress through the building. I took up the hurricane lamp and started up the stairs again. It was annoying, though, to note, at each step I took upward, that what I lost in anger, I gained in anxiety and dread.

Two

By the time I reached the second floor once more, I had no doubt my silent comrade in the attic was following all my movements attentively. Whoever he was, he couldn't help hearing me. Even when I walked on my toes the board floors creaked. The door of the narrow white staircase to the attic was at the front of the hall, opposite Sybil Thursten's bedroom. The door itself was so unobtrusive I almost missed it, and when I was climbing those tricky triangular stairs, I kept wondering what I would do if something absolutely inexplicable met me at the top. Like Sybil Thursten's ghost. An idiotic thought, again, but I was so nervous I would not have been too surprised to see her there.

As a matter of fact, nothing met me at the top of the stairs except clean salt air, which had no business there after five months. The low-ceilinged attic rooms and the little hall were charming, even in the flickering light of my hurricane lamp. I stood there thoughtfully in the hall, considering the closed doors on the west side of the house, guessing the back rooms would be full of the usual fascinating rubbish found in old houses. I decided the middle room on the west side was the one I had come to investigate. I stalked across the crackling boards of the floor, put my free hand on the doorknob, and tried it as silently as possible. The door was not locked. I inhaled deeply to reinforce my courage and then opened the door.

The room was inhabited, but it was hard for me to believe those first few seconds that its inhabitant was alive. She sat in a large, uncompromising armchair across the room, her stern, lined features etched by the cruel glow of sunset, her pale eyes glaring at me like fire seen behind frosted glass. She was Sybil Thursten's mother, the redoubtable Mrs. Ada Jeffrey, and I needed no more than this first exchange of looks between us to know how much she hated me.

I nearly groveled in my effort to soften the bitter, vengeful woman. "I'm so sorry, Mrs. Jeffrey. I didn't mean to burst in on you like this. Did I startle you?"

The woman's deep voice, with its arrogant Mayfair accent, which she had preserved for forty years in an alien land, managed to cut me down with its first words.

"It would be impossible for someone like

you to startle me, young woman. Furthermore, even if I had been as impressionable as the Nisei in the jury, I would have heard those noisy feet of yours clambering through my daughter's house."

I swallowed hard, remembered her bereavement and made allowances. "Mr. Thursten is coming out to Beach House tomorrow. He asked me to get things a bit presentable. Everything was so dusty . . ."

"Not my daughter's room."

"No, no. Not her room," I agreed hastily. "You've—it's been kept beautifully."

"Naturally. I have kept it so. I suppose you will be leaving when you have finished waving your precious dust sheets out the windows."

I agreed, without much grace, that once my work was done I would not be invited here again unless Mark wished to conduct the shipping business from his home. No need to tell her that Mark hadn't mentioned my doing the dust maid's work. That had been my own idea. He had merely asked me to see what needed to be done to open the house.

The burning light in Mrs. Jeffrey's eyes seemed to be a trifle subdued now, probably because the sun had gone down behind the ragged coastline, leaving it in picturesque black silhouette against the pale sky.

"I see. For your information, Mark is at this moment in the process of inviting me, and my daughter, of course, to remain here for the immediate future."

It shook me to have her mention her "daughter," until I realized that she was speaking not of the dead Sybil but of her younger sister, Carol. I said, "How nice! I hope—"

"Yes, yes." Mrs. Jeffrey waved aside my half-expressed fears impatiently. "All is forgiven. We now believe, Carol and I . . . and little Bobbie, that someone else murdered my daughter." She paused just long enough so that I would connect this remark with her next. "You must come and stay also, Miss—ah—Carter. You will be a companion to Carol, and you may be of help with young Bobbie. She is a curiously unstable child, much too fond of knives and scissors. That sort of thing."

I found the hurricane lamp moist under my perspiring fingers and I tried to beg off from this ominous invitation, but she was surprisingly persistent.

"You are a competent girl in your way. I see no insurmountable reason why you would not fit in. Temporarily, at least." She looked me up and down like a buyer in a slave mart. "Play down some of those overripe looks of yours, girl. You want Carol to like you. And Bobbie, of course." She waved me off.

I started to leave but couldn't resist adding ironically, "And you, too, I want to like me, Mrs. Jeffrey."

She smiled, a singularly humorless grimace, showing too-perfect and too-white teeth.

"Of course. But then, you must know, after my invitation, how very essential your presence will be." She added, as I left abruptly, "Don't worry about my food tonight. I have already eaten."

Charming creature! It gave me a decidedly creepy feeling to know, as I went about completing my work in the house, that the old basilisk was up there in the attic room, doubtless aware of every step I took, guessing my fear and playing on it. I decided to drive back to Honolulu when I finished, no matter how late the hour might be.

And what was this plan of hers, for which I was essential? Was it possible, since she said she no longer suspected her son-in-law of Sybil's death, that she now suspected me? God forbid!

Meanwhile, however, I wanted at least to have the master bedroom and the first floor sufficiently dusted so they wouldn't depress Mark when he arrived tomorrow. I finally worked my way down to the large first-floor lanai, and having dusted off the furniture and swept the mat rug, I went outside to shake my dust mop and cloths, feeling the cool moisture of evening damp on my bare legs below the shorts I wore. Every time I stood on those wooden stairs above the beach, I remembered Sybil Thursten's death and agreed with my first conclusion, that she must have been singularly clumsy to have killed herself from this place. It would take an extraordinary fall from here for her to have struck her forehead on the little coral cropping.

But in this line of thought there were more horrors. The only alternative *was* murder; since Mark had not killed her, who had? I shivered and went down the steps. As I touched the beach, and my feet sank into the cooling sand, I remembered Mrs. Jeffrey's nasty remarks about my noisy feet and how I was too "overripe" for her younger daughter. I suppose she referred to my hair which is like her daughters', dark blonde, but I wore it freer than Carol. I got occasional jobs doing television commercials because of my hair, and oddly enough, considering Mrs. Jeffrey's implied criticism, I'd done some hosiery ads. Long legs were an asset in spite of Mrs. Jeffrey!

It was a slight though not unpleasant shock to see in the dim light someone strolling along the gleaming wet beach a little distance to the west. At least, I thought, there was another human being besides me out here on these desolate shores. The walker came nearer. I pretended to be looking around the house at the windblown sand while I decided that the slight black-clad figure walking close to the foaming breakers was a male with tousled black hair and a raffish look. If he were only unshaven, I thought cynically, he might be the ideal beachcomber. Even at a distance he looked pale, though, like an indoor man. Curious, to find him wandering along this coast. He wasn't the typical malihini from the mainland. I hadn't the least idea why he made me vaguely uneasy, except that he seemed so out of place.

I shook my dust cloths, and coughing a bit under the backlash of dust, moved blindly out toward the beach to escape the cloud. I was just raising my dust mop to shake it again when my foot, feeling for something firm, suddenly encountered space where there had been solid wet sand.

It was my own fault, naturally. I had been too busy wondering what the unlikely stranger was doing on the Thursten sector of this isolated beach. Now, before I could recover from that step into space, I fell across a camouflaged hole in the sand. It was an *imu*, one of those pits generally lined with *ti* leaves and hot rocks for the baking of a pig, the succulent main course at a luau. My leg plunged into the pit as far as my knee, and I felt a terrific wrench of pain, which, however, did not bother me as much as finding myself in this ridiculous sprawl across the little pit.

I said a few things under my breath while trying to brace myself on the edges of the pit firmly enough to pull my leg out. I suppose the sharp twinges of pain robbed me of strength, and after several efforts, I groaned and stopped, hoping the stranger I had seen would come to my assistance. Why he hadn't done so before now was pretty frightening in itself. He could hardly have avoided seeing my accident. I twisted the upper half of my body around to see what had happened to him. My partly formed suspicions were confirmed. He was standing close to the edge of the pit, the dark eyes in his pale face looking down at me in the most curious, speculative way, and with no sympathy whatever.

"If it's not too much trouble, would you mind giving me a hand?" I managed to ask him with all the irony I could muster.

"Certainly. No trouble at all." His smile might have been attractive, except for an odd twist of—malice? He had a definite accent, a brogue, I thought. While it was more Irish or Welsh than Mrs. Jeffrey's, the reminder gave me chills.

He took my hands and began to pull me up, not too gently. I screamed. We immediately found ourselves at an impasse, with my injured leg half in and half out of the pit, while the rest of me was kneeling, my shorts torn and bloody, one bare thigh gritty with clinging wet sand, the other ugly with scratches and streaks of blood.

"Are you going to leave me dangling here all night?" I demanded.

27

He reminded me with exaggerated patience and formality, "You screamed, madam!"

"Ignore it."

This time, with a strength surprising for one so slender, he lifted me out onto the sand, where I crouched over my poor messy leg, trying not to cry. He stood up and looked around, studying the big Beach House, whose shadow still hovered over us in the blue dusk.

"You come from there, I suppose." He sighed. "Naturally, you want to be carried."

I gritted my teeth, but there was no point in taking offense until I had hobbled safely to wherever I could get help.

"Just let me use you as a crutch." It was all he was worth, anyway. It seemed to me he might be enjoying my pain. What was he? A sadist?

Silently, he took my arm and we started off, with me limping. Then I remembered the dust mop, stopped, and painfully stooped to pick it up. I was beginning to suspect no bones were broken, but there were muscles pulled, the one running up the back of my leg—whatever that was—and my ankle was either sprained or badly strained. Also, there were those bloody scratches.

If the lights weren't on yet in the Beach House, the telephone probably wouldn't be working either, but at the moment all I was looking for was a cushiony place where I could sit down and stop shaking. What with the frozen hatred of the woman on the top floor of the house, and the charming malice of my unwilling rescuer, I hardly felt safe anywhere.

He did get me up the outside stairs and into the lanai, however, and as I had left the hurricane lamp there, the screened porch looked a little more cheerful than the ominous and growing darkness out on the beach. I limped to the old couch, sank down on top of the afghan, and motioned the Irishman, or whatever he was, that he was free to go away.

But he wasn't looking at me. He was staring at the ceiling. I had an odd notion he knew Mrs. Jeffrey was upstairs. Certainly, with her curiosity, she must know what had happened to me, and that this stranger—if he was a stranger to her—was here in the house.

Too nervous to deal with him, I said, "I appreciate your help, mister—whoever you are. But I can manage. You needn't stay." I began to rub my leg hard, hoping to conquer pain with pain, and when I looked up, the curious stranger, who had been so singularly incurious about me, was gone. He had behaved almost like a phantom. I didn't even hear him close the door or go down the stairs onto the sand.

When I was sure I was alone, I huddled myself into the afghan and sat there until the shivering passed. The sunset wind had died down and the air felt warm and damp, but my flesh

29

was still cold. Finally, when I felt more myself again, I moved my legs out from under the afghan and stretched them. They had grown stiff, and the sore one ached in a fiery way, but the bloody scratches seemed on examination to be very slight. That was a relief. And the sprain, while it ached, was not as painful as the less important pull of the muscles.

"Well, I'll live, anyway," I thought, and began to consider what to do next. I would have to get something done about my leg, but right now I simply didn't have the energy. And meanwhile, as I sat there at one end of the lanai, this insufferable house seemed to be very much aware of me. I could hear cracking sounds all over the building. Just as I was calming down, almost relaxed enough to close my eyes briefly, there was a terrifically sharp crack at my ear. I jumped several inches and twisted around to see what threatened me, and incidentally gave my sore leg an extra twist. I saw nothing threatening in the immediate vicinity of my flickering lamp, but it was impossible to make out anything in the huge room beyond. The noise had undoubtedly come from the settling of the ancient walls. Still ... it was equally unsettling to sense that both the strange people I had met at Beach House tonight appeared to hate me. I could understand and even, in an odd way, sympathize with Mrs. Jeffrey's feelings. She clearly connected me with my employer's escape from "justice," or her weird idea of justice. Since she must have suffered greatly from her daughter's death, I could make allowances even while I made up my mind to stay out of her claws.

But that other weird creature, who had at one point appeared to be a slight and attractive male, now seemed to me to have been a malign phantom with a perverted sense of humor. I got up and limped painfully to the door, which had been left unlocked. I wasn't even sure the fellow had gone out by anything as prosaic as a door. His departure was more in the nature of a disappearance.

Since I was on my feet, I thought I might as well try my luck with the telephone, check Mark's study for neatness, and see if there was a bite to eat or a drop to drink while I spent another hour recuperating before I ventured out to my car. I knew that in the car I had some band-aids and salve, which would be better than nothing to ward off infection. I took the lamp with me and limped toward the kitchen, passing the study on my left. It was a tiny room (I had spent much of my four previous visits to Beach House in that room, typing up reports and bringing Mark's shipping schedules up-to-date), but it apparently suited Mark, and seemed cozy in a masculine, book-and-leather way. I tried the doorknob and was surprised to find the room locked.

I had only one key with me, so the condition of the room would have to remain as it had been since the day Mark had left it on his way to his lawyers' offices in Honolulu. Still, I wondered about the locked door as I limped on down the hall to the kitchen. Since Mrs. Jeffrey was in the house, how could I be sure she had not been in the room herself and locked the door for reasons of her own? Surely Mark would have given me the key to the study door if he had locked it himself. He had particularly asked me to air out that room.

There was a telephone extension in the hall and I picked up the phone, but the line was dead. An unexpected breeze made the lamplight flicker, so I moved as quickly as I could to the kitchen, whose prosaic layout and contents hardly seemed suited to phantoms. I found a bottle of Dry Sack Sherry over in one corner of the sink board and saw that a third of it was gone. A stemmed crystal glass with the Jeffrey crest was set beside it; this was obviously Mrs. Jeffrey's property, and the harmless tippling made her seem almost human.

I was still enough in awe of her to get another and plainer glass from the cupboard before I poured myself a drink, though. It would be the last straw in her hatred of me, I thought, if I broke some of her good crystal. The sherry warmed me so quickly and so adequately I could almost feel it rushing to my toes. I turned away from the sink with a sense of well-being.

Standing so close behind me that I almost stepped on her properly shod foot was the wrinkled but imperious Mrs. Jeffrey. She was smiling, but the glint in her pale eyes was tigerish.

"Do have some more. There's the good girl. You've been overdoing. You need— Here. Let me pour."

Three

I barely stifled a scream. The annoying ache of my leg and the jar of my fall, which had affected my nerves, made me overreact now at the unexpected sight of her. I felt sure she had gotten a great deal of satisfaction out of startling me. She took the sherry bottle from my still fingers and started to pour, although my little glass was already three-quarters full.

"Please. I've got enough here. Mrs. Jeffrey, I don't need any—"

"Don't be silly, girl. After that nasty fall you took, this is just the thing to settle your nerves. My younger daughter has what we used to call in my day an extreme irritation of the nerves, and a glass of sherry does much more for her than those disgusting Martinis everyone drinks."

"Martinis are passé," I muttered, as if it was important to put her down some way. "Have you tried any Canadian Club lately?"

She ignored this, as well she might. I was

only trying to establish that her hold over me could be broken, that I was less afraid of her. Nevertheless, I found myself sipping the sherry to get its warmth and false courage, while she watched me with extraordinary interest. When I finished the glass she tried to persuade me to drink another. That failing, when I said I would have to drive to the closest village and look for a doctor, she said abruptly, "Don't be ridiculous! You must come now and sit down somewhere comfortably, and I will bandage that ankle of yours. You may have a bad sprain." She looked around like a busy house-keeper. "Let me see. . . . You will need a disin-fectant. Some of those tiny bandages for your cuts, and— Leave everything to me. Here, I'll help you into the living room. There is a couch. You will want to lie down."

This was a far cry, indeed, from her original conduct to me upstairs, and I couldn't begin to guess why she had changed toward me. If she really had.

"No, I won't. Really. I've got to be getting back to town."

But it was no use. My knee hurt. I had the feeling I was on an endless treadmill and couldn't get out of this place if I wanted to now. The elegant old witch had me under a spell. Probably the sherry was instrumental: she sensed all this, I knew. She went along with me through the house, her stiff gold hostess

35

gown brushing the floor behind us, making a funny little sound like chattery whispers. I even got to the point where I looked over my shoulder, but in spite of the darkness that closed in quickly behind us as we moved forward, there seemed to be no danger lurking. No visible danger.

We passed the door to Mark's study and I said suddenly, "I could rest in here. It's out of the way, and I know the room."

Were my suspicions too sharply acute, or did she actually hesitate in a second or two of panic?

"No, girl. It's not comfortable at all. Sybil always said it was so small she got claustrophobia when she entered. Sybil had a very comfortable chair here in the living room. I think it will do nicely for you while I get a few things together to bandage you properly."

I was still protesting, though vaguely, when she backed me into a big cushioned armchair which was placed, perversely, almost in the center of the room, along with an old-fashioned but rather charming little round maple table with a lamp. They acted as room dividers, along with a couch facing the clean, empty fireplace. Unfortunately for anyone like me, cursed with an imagination, chairs placed with their backs to a room always gave me the creepy sensation that "things" were stealing up behind me. This seemed even more likely when I found myself alone in the big chair with my foot up on a hassock, and my chilled bare arms hugged by the very arms of the chair that had, not too long ago, caressed the mistress of the house, Sybil Thursten. The sherry had made me sleepy, though, and my pain subsided while I rested. But two or three minutes at a time were all I could stand before I sneaked a nervous look over the arm of the chair, sure that I heard whispered voices somewhere not far from this room.

I saw nothing except the shadowy, unfamiliar shapes of the furniture, and beyond, the open doorway to the darkness that was the lanai. I had locked the outside door, hadn't I? I studied the furniture again, discussing very unemotionally with myself how strange it was that unfamiliar furnishings in a nearly dark room can so easily resemble faces and huddled bodies.

And while I was trying to find answers to unsolved riddles, what had really happened to my shadowy and unwilling rescuer? It was curious about that *imu* so carefully covered over by twigs, giant leaves, and a residue of sand. Some fool had disguised it so neatly I could have killed myself. Or at the very least, maimed myself. Some people were being awfully careless and thoughtless about life and limbs around here. Or were they merely careless?

From that I began to worry about Mrs.

Jeffrey's sherry. Was it only because I had drunk it on an empty stomach that I now felt so weak, so sleepy? I sat up, shook myself, and rubbed my sore leg, hoping the painful pressure would snap me out of this lethargy.

If only it were tomorrow night! Mark would be here. And his staff. What a difference that would make! Just seeing Mark's rocky, stern face with its rare smile would be enough for me.

As if there were spidery little antennae growing out of her imperious white head, Mrs. Jeffrey must have sensed my growing suspicion. I heard her rustling skirt before her disembodied form managed to materialize in the doorway from the hall. Although the basilisk eyes glinted as they caught the candlelight, she was undeniably on an errand of mercy. She carried on a monkeypod tray a roll of gauze, a tube of ointment, some peroxide, band-aids and adhesive tape. I had been half expecting her to show up at the very least with Lady Macbeth's dagger. The small blunt-ended scissors were hardly a substitute as worthy of those eyes of hers.

"How is the leg? Stiff, of course. They always are." She set her first aid material on the little maple table and pulled up another hassock. I was impressed by her systematic approach to my injuries. Common sense told me if she had been poisoning the sherry and disguising *imus* so that I would break my neck, she wouldn't be helping me now. And she was very good at the job she had undertaken for me. My ankle felt a thousand times better with its stiff, clean, antiseptic bandage, and even the sting of those bloody little scratches on my leg was refreshing.

"I've eaten, girl," she reminded me as she picked up her materials, "but you will have to have something yourself. You're shockingly thin."

From Mrs. Jeffrey I accepted this as the straightforward, honest observation of someone who did not intend it as a compliment.

"I'll eat in town, Mrs. Jeffrey. I shouldn't have stayed this long. I meant to leave an hour ago."

"That would be most unwise. And then too, you are the first human being I have seen since those noisy university students left this afternoon." She had started across the room, the beginning of one of those disembodying acts of hers, when she looked around at me. "I must confess, this old house is not the most reassuring place to spend the night alone." She smiled grimly. "Now, am I to be trusted?"

"Certainly, ma'am. I only thought—" Completely tongue-tied, I stumbled around to find an excuse for leaving, but the truth was, I had never felt less like walking out to my car and making a long drive. I took a breath and plunged in. "Mrs. Jeffrey, I know you felt I was wrong in testifying, but I had to tell the truth. Mr. Thursten *was* in the office talking to me on my birthday, just as I said in court. Besides, he loved your daughter very much."

"Bosh!" said the old lady surprisingly. "Everyone loved Sybil. There wasn't a man in the Islands who wouldn't have married my daughter, but she chose that—that chunk of granite. That hard, cold— Never mind! It's nothing to do with you . . . I hope!"

"Really, Mrs. Jeffrey, I am only hired by the Thursten Shipping Company. Just like the rest of the staff. Meanwhile, though, I should go back to my apartment. I wasn't given permission to spend the night here."

I watched her vanish into the darkness down the hall, but I had barely gotten to my feet and started trying out my bandaged leg when she returned. She had put away her nursing equipment and came in now to suggest that various items in the kitchen might be pleasing for my supper. Before I could make her believe that I really did not intend to stay she came rustling toward me, slightly suggestive of a rattler giving warning in a spirit of fair play.

"But you misunderstand. I wish you to stay. You will keep me company in this old house. You, young and healthy, you will frighten off the things I see at night when I am alone."

"Things you—see?" I managed feebly.

40

She shrugged; startlingly enough, she looked and sounded sincere. "My poor Sybil. She seems very close to me these nights. She wouldn't hurt you, you know. You might sleep in her own bed—and she would not hurt you." I must have looked my doubt because she added, this time with unmistakable irony, "Not unless it was you who struck and killed her, and you have said it was not. So you can have no fear of her, even though she is dead."

"Thank you. But I really do have to get back to town."

I picked up the lamp and hobbled toward the kitchen door, which was nearest the place where I had parked my car. Even with the lamp I found it no easy job to make my way around furniture that was out of place, or to avoid unexpected wavering shadows just at the periphery of my vision. I marveled that Mrs. Jeffrey got around so well with no more than the flashlight that I saw balanced on the newel-post of the stairs.

She made no further move to stop me, and I set the lamp on the sink and went outside, relieved to find the stars were out, and the moon was coming up. The sand and the long, ragged shoreline gleamed in the light. I limped through deep sand to my old Chevrolet under the *hau* tree and tried my key in the door, but it was already unlocked. I had been careless as usual. I got in behind the wheel, painfully favoring my sore leg, and turned the key in the ignition. Nothing happened. I tried again, a little panicked. Not even a flooded motor. Just no response. Now, what had I done wrong?

I got out, and more or less as a defiant gesture, raised the hood and stared at the motor, about as useless an act as I was capable of, because I don't know one end of a motor from the other. Anyway, it wouldn't go. I leaned against the car a full minute or two, wondering if Mrs. Jeffrey could have put my car out of commission sometime this evening, for instance while I was wrestling with that *imu* out on the beach. But it was not her sort of weapon. I had heard that she traveled around Honolulu in a chauffeured car when she traveled at all.

I looked over and down from the dirt road at the west side of Beach House. There was a faint light in one of the attic rooms, in the room, I thought at first, where I had found Mrs. Jeffrey this afternoon. I squinted to be sure as I counted the windows. No, the light was coming from a room further toward the back of the house. What on earth was she doing, exploring the place room by room? And if so, what did she hope to find?

It didn't seem reasonable that she had tampered with my car; yet, quite obviously, she wanted me to stay at Beach House tonight. Unless her purpose was sinister enough to involve murder, why would she go to such trouble to keep me here? I really wasn't gullible enough to believe that the house itself frightened her.

On the spur of the moment, I made up my mind to spite the old lady and walk to the nearest village for help with my car. The flesh of my bare legs and arms was cold and damp with the sea air; I got an old terry-cloth poncho out of the trunk of my car, slipped it over my head, and tied it around my waist. It warmed me surprisingly, considering it had no sleeves and barely reached my knees. I remembered to lock the car this time and began my walk in the dark between the great hibiscus hedges and under the gaunt, tortured limbs of the tropic foliage that everywhere around me shivered in the breeze and reached out tentative, groping fingers toward me.

I had seen no human being since I limped away from Beach House, and yet my imagination kept me constantly looking around to discover who was stalking me. I stopped and leaned against the grotesque, crawling roots of an ancient tree and rubbed my sore leg while I tried to see into the darkness of the jungle growth on the upper, *mauka* side of the road, away from the ocean breakers and the beach. It was still early enough for farmers tending their papaya trees to be in those fields beyond the growth, but I couldn't make out anything I thought might be human—until I turned and looked over my shoulder at the edge of the beach below, where a little coral reef projected into the foaming surf, and this time, in the moonlight, I was sure I saw the black figure of the phantom beachcomber. Something like glass or metal shone in his hand, and in my present state I thought at once of a knife or a gun. He appeared to be solidly human until the moon went under a fleecy little cloud and the beachcomber, having reverted to his phantom state, vanished again.

I was sure he had seen me. He was facing in my direction, and if he had gone behind that coral reef he could possibly head me off further along the road—he and that shiny thing in his hand. It was no use. I was too scared, too tired to go further. I began to stumble back toward Beach House. Better to face the known danger of the old woman at the house than the unknown phantom with his most unghostly weapon.

I still hadn't the least notion why he threatened me, but one thing was being made very clear: when I told the truth on the witness stand, I must have made some singularly unpleasant enemies. Then I reasoned that Mark, as an island power, rich and successful, was probably the real target of this enmity, and that I had doubtless merely come between him and the destruction his enemies craved. For the first time I wondered if Sybil Thursten's death had been arranged with this very destruction in mind.

It is amazing how fear can overcome aches and pains. I came back in sight of the big, ugly house almost before I was ready for it, and as I passed my stalled car, I wondered if it might be safer to spend the night here, maybe curled up in the back seat. But I kept thinking how eerie it would be to wake up and see some strange face staring in at me through the windows. I shivered and decided I preferred the Beach House with its probably imaginary terrors. Besides, and this may have influenced me in a practical way, I was absolutely starving. I hadn't eaten since a quick brunch at eleven that morning. I began to think better of Mrs. Jeffrey's suggested supper, to be whipped up from whatever cans were available in the kitchen cupboards of Beach House. At least, I no longer was absurdly afraid of being poisoned. Mrs. Jeffrey had had her chance to do that with the sherry, and hadn't come through.

I tried the back door into the old-fashioned entry. Mrs. Jeffrey had not locked it. Either she had no fear of burglaries, or she was very sure of my return. I limped into the kitchen, dropped down on a quaint, not unattractive ladder-backed chair, and heard myself let out a sound between a groan and a sob. I was close to crying anyway. I was so damnably tired and hungry and scared. And along with all that, I was depressed because this house wasn't nearly the way I wanted it to be for Mark. Mark should have a grand, masculine house. Or even better, a severe but splendid castle. That would fit his rugged look, his strength, his brooding sadness and long silences . . . his smile. . . . I was amused at my romantic view of my employer.

I found a wall can opener and ground open a can of consommé madrilene and then a can of beans, and unearthed some big crackers with sesame seeds. I was so hungry it was a feast. Mrs. Jeffrey came down to see me finish a glass of papaya juice, feeling infinitely better. I said gaily, "Hi, Mrs. Jeffrey!" sounding so cheerful she glanced with suspicion at the Dry Sack Sherry bottle.

She said, "So you've decided to be sensible! Good. If you want to lie down and rest that ankle of yours, I've no objection to your borrowing my daughter's room. I'll turn down the spread and see that there are fresh towels."

"No!" I said it so quickly we both jumped. "I mean, Mr. Thursten wouldn't like it at all. He never likes anyone to touch her things."

"So I am told," she remarked with her grim, unpleasant smile. "Still, he need not know."

But I was firm on that point, and when she found I intended to curl up on the couch in the lanai, she seemed suspicious that it was some false modesty of mine that made me refuse to sleep in one of the well-furnished bedrooms. But my private reason was that if anything weird did happen, I wanted to be someplace handy to run from, sore ankle and all. I had no intention of being trapped in the very place most likely to be "visited" by the dead woman I had so envied in life.

"Very well, then. Would you care to borrow sleeping garments? My daughter"—at my quick look she corrected herself, though I was sure she had deliberately tried to startle me—"my younger daughter, Carol, left pajamas, a nightgown or two, and some robes here."

I refused these as well. I had been told a year ago that Carol had been set for my job as Mark's secretary, but I was hired instead because I had faster shorthand. Carol would hardly be any more anxious than her sister Sybil to loan me her night clothes.

"Well, then, Miss Carter, if you insist. However, you may find it lonely out on the lanai all night with nothing but screens between you and the elements."

I shrugged. "Just as long as that nasty dark-haired beachcomber doesn't come prowling around here again I'll be all right."

The old woman looked at me with a kind of inner stillness I could almost feel.

"What beachcomber is this?"

"The fellow who—very reluctantly—helped me out of that pit down the beach."

47

"My dear girl, I saw you stumble over the *imu*. No one helped you out. You managed very well, I must say." Mrs. Jeffrey turned away as if she suspected me of making up the whole tale.

"Now, look here!" I exclaimed, raising my voice in an unpleasant way that made her face twitch, as if she found these sounds unbearable to her delicate ears. "There was too a man. A beachcomber, I think. He had on a black pullover with a turtleneck and black slacks and dark eyes and a pale face."

"What happened then to this extraordinary vision?"

That was the embarrassing part. "He just disappeared," I tendered lamely.

"I should imagine he did precisely that," she agreed in the irritating, sardonic voice that made a lie out of everything I said. "Go and rest, girl. You badly need it." And she left me.

The really uncomfortable thing was that her all-knowing assurance proved contagious. The dark-eyed beachcomber's behavior had been exceedingly odd from start to finish. Was he, after all, just something I had *imagined?* At any other time, the idea would have been absurd. But tonight, in my present state, almost anything seemed possible.

Four

It was well after nine o'clock when I huddled down on the lanai couch between a pair of crisp sheets with the afghan on top. There was a loose spring jabbing me in the stomach, so I curled around it and reached out for the hurricane lamp. I had put a new candle in, the other having burned down to splotches of tallow, and now I debated whether to blow out the lamp or let it burn through the night.

I felt a little silly about this, but the real question was whether I preferred to see any possible intruder, and be seen in the process, or to rely on the darkness to make me invisible, and the intruder, if any, also invisible. I decided on the darkness, figuring I would soon get used to seeing in the dark, especially with the help of all that starlight on the beach.

I got up on one elbow, looked all around me, saw nothing, of course, and removed the glass protector long enough to snuff the candle. I had the book of matches on the floor at my fingertips and I set the still-hot lamp beside it, just in case. Once the light was out and my eyes had gotten used to the semidarkness, it was easier to see out of the screens on three sides of the lanai. The moonlight came and went, depending on vagrant clouds, providing, along with the stars, more light outside along the desolate beach than inside where I was. This suited me very well. I didn't want any phantom beachcombers prowling around those screens without my knowing it.

While the house cooled and crackled in the dark, I wondered about the ambivalence of Mrs. Jeffrey. She had deliberately tried to frighten me by adding to my own fear that the beachcomber was unreal, and yet this woman had gone to some effort to make me comfortable. No doubt, once I was maneuvered into remaining at Beach House, she might well try to make me suffer for having testified at Mark's trial. Yet surely a woman of her intelligence would turn her suspicions elsewhere, if she did believe it was impossible for Mark to have killed her daughter.

I sat up on the couch and smiled at my own naïveté. Probably she had done just that. Somehow, she had convinced herself that I was the alternative suspect. In my vague state between alarm and anger this afternoon, I had sensed something of this switch in her suspicions. She doubtless still thought I had lied about the time I had seen Mark that day, but now she must think I had lied to shield myself. Or worse, she thought we were in it together.

Having decided to blame Mrs. Jeffrey for every disaster that had overpowered me this evening, including the off-again, on-again beach phantom, I settled down to calm my punished nerves and get some sleep. Clearly, she was not out to "get me" right away, anyway.

Considering all the things I had to worry about, I went to sleep with a promptness that was heroic, as I look back on it. I had unpleasant dreams, somewhat like those I've known after eating pizzas at midnight. It wasn't surprising, because I had eaten a meal as heterogeneous as my dreams. Mostly, though, in this little chain of nightmares, I was climbing stairs in the dark. I was always climbing stairs somewhere in these dreams, feeling my way as if my life depended on it. Maybe it did. I still remember with what dread I made my tired legs move up each stair, although the distance seemed to increase until I was moaning with the effort.

I woke myself up with a groan, and my first conscious reaction was embarrassment. I devoutly hoped no one had heard me. I was breathing hard, and was worried by the silly nightmare's hold on me. It wasn't as if the idea of incessantly climbing stairs had some meaning. My ex-friends in Los Angeles would have read some Freudian sexual symbol in it, but to me it meant nothing now save for its having tired me out and reminded me of my injured leg, which managed to ache and to sting at the same time.

At least I didn't make the usual mistake of those who wake up in strange places. I knew exactly where I was, and I sat up, shaking myself, beginning to wonder if any outside force had influenced my idiotic nightmare. The silence everywhere was so noticeable I imagined it crowding against the screens, and only a minute or two later realized this oppressive silence was caused by the receding tide and the temporary letup of the breeze. I yawned and supposed it must be near dawn. The thought of this relieved me. The sooner I got through this night the better. I looked at my wristwatch and then shook it impatiently. By the faint starlight seeping through the screens, I read that it was 11:25, which was ridiculous. My watch must have stopped. It had to be near dawn. It took me several seconds with the watch at my ear before I realized the watch hadn't stopped at all. There were still hours before daylight, when I could really feel safe.

The trouble was, my first impetus to sleep had gone. I had slept off the aching tiredness that wrapped itself close to me like my worn-out poncho, and now, try as I would, I couldn't seem to stop the nervous, throbbing awareness all over my body, the awful, cowardly prickle of fear. And there wasn't, at the moment, a thing to cause or to explain it. I shook myself, decided I had been too warm, and kicked off the afghan. My sore leg was so stiff I could hardly move it without crying out, but at least I had managed to change my position and should be more comfortable.

Or I thought I was.

I had barely closed my eyes when the screens surrounding the lanai began to rattle with a faint ebb and flow of rhythm. My common sense told me this was the night breeze sweeping again toward the house, but the realization didn't keep my eyes from snapping open and staring anxiously at the screen across the room from me. There was still considerable starlight outside, and its reflection from the beach put the exterior of the house in bright relief. By contrast, I hoped I was invisible, but the light sifted in, and as I looked around the room I began to recognize various objects of furniture, including my couch.

The persistent rattle, followed by the low whine—or was it a moan?—of the freshening sea breeze through the screen caught at my nerves again and I leaned forward, frowning hard to make out anything at the far screen across the room.

"Of course there isn't anything, you idiot!" I told myself with angry impatience, and turned

53

my attention from that side of the room to the screens on either side of the door. Beyond that door were the wooden steps, those innocent, perfectly simple steps that somehow had killed Sybil Thursten. The screens looked as innocent as the steps.

There was only one part of the room I hadn't been concerned about, but the screened wall above my bed was so silent that not even the sea breeze disturbed it. It must have been this stillness that crept into my consciousness at last. I twisted around to look up. The screen was close enough so that, sitting up on the couch as I was, I could touch it with my outspread fingers. Although I had moved suddenly, I had no particular motive, no sense of immediate danger. It was simply that the wall of the room, directly behind my couch, was the last place to be checked.

Beyond that screen, faintly shimmering in the starlight there was something peering in at me. I blinked while my world seemed to stop, and even the sea wind was still. Curiously enough, it took me several seconds before the full horror of what I saw crept over me. It seemed to be a human face, but the silvered features were so pallid they made me think of something that had lain on the bottom of the sea. I couldn't see them clearly, but they looked familiar— frighteningly familiar. The small but arrogant

54

nose, the silky dark blonde hair, the pale eyes and sulky mouth almost as pale . . .

It was the dead Sybil Thursten.

I thought I was going to scream, but my vocal cords were paralyzed. They felt stiff as dry leather in my throat. I just stared at the thing until my body began to shiver. At least I recovered my wits and a little of my courage. I scrambled off the couch, forcing my body pressure painfully on my sore leg, and rushed to the screen door. The lock was stubborn, or maybe it was my trembling fingers, but I finally got it open and then stopped practically on the edge of the top step. I didn't want to follow literally in the steps of Sybil Thursten.

As I went down the steps with care, I tried to see around the corner of the big house. Hardly more than a minute had gone by since I had seen the dead woman's face peering down at me through the time-blackened screen, but I only half expected to see the creature. Twenty or thirty seconds with my back to the thing were enough to convince me that what I had seen was probably someone masquerading as Sybil Thursten—but that hideous resemblance! Was it a real apparition? In either case, it wasn't likely to hang around waiting for me.

It was much darker at the east side of the house than I had bargained for, and I kept thinking of foolish women who got knocked in the head and worse, because they wandered around in the dark. I stopped under the screened lanai. Where the ghostly Sybil had been, there was nothing. The starlight was not bright enough for me to make out any footprints except my own. The sand looked the way it always did, all pocked with little scooped-out places, blown into hollows by the intermittent sea breeze.

I looked around again, shivering. The wind had started up with a gloomy moan. The long, desolate beach was still deserted, but the narrow, darker section east of the house was shadowed by the partially completed garage up a hundred yards from the house, and by the rugged low cliff that marked the eastern end of the beach. Up on the road, beyond the garage and the cliff, I suddenly saw something move. Dark as it was up there, I couldn't dismiss that figure as a lively figment of my nightmares. I had lost all my curiosity now, and wanted only to get back to what I for the moment thought of as the safety of Beach House.

I limped rapidly along the side wall of the house, but as I turned the corner and headed for the stairs I heard running feet, and turned in terror to see someone moving swiftly across the sand toward me, someone much too big to be any phantom of Sybil Thursten. I forgot the pain of my ankle and ran for the stairs, stumbling and scratching my way up until I reached the doorknob and pulled myself erect. The wind was moaning past my ears, obliterating other sounds, but I had barely gotten inside the lanai when I felt a pressure, very strong, pushing the door open again. Panicked, I yelled, "Let go! Go away! Get out."

There was a hard thrust, rocking me backward against the couch, and a second or two later a hard, uncompromising hand closed firmly over my mouth. I suppose I must have screamed, though I don't remember doing so. Then I heard Mark Thursten's half-exasperated, half-amused voice in the darkness.

"Livia? What the devil are you doing running around the beach at midnight screaming your head off? Are you all right now? Can I count on your not rousing the household?" My employer took his hands off me. "Confound it! Where is the light switch?"

I heard a sickening sound like the clash of bone against a wooden table leg, and felt even worse than he must have.

"Mark! I'm terribly sorry. I'll get this lamp lit. The electricity isn't on yet. Just sit tight."

He had been about to groan, I'm sure, but he said instead, "That's about all I can do. Sit— or limp—tight."

When I got the hurricane lamp lighted, I couldn't help laughing. There in front of me was the man who had come to encompass my whole life, unknown to himself, and this rugged, tall, self-possessed man was rubbing his pants leg along the thigh, and wrinkling his aquiline nose at the pain.

"I suppose it's funny, but I'm damned if I see why," he told me, but I thought his eyes looked amused.

I pointed to the bandages and band-aids that liberally decorated my bare leg, and this time, instead of laughing as I had hoped he might, he reacted in an even better way. He was concerned.

"What happened? Livia! Don't tell me you fell over the same table leg! I'm sorry I startled you, but I was so surprised to see someone flitting over the beach in that ghostly way, I didn't know what to think. I had to catch you before you vanished in a clap of fog. Or whatever. Are you all right?"

"Fine. Don't worry about me," I assured him, pleased, at least, that he cared if I battered myself up. My biggest triumph had been the magic moment four months ago when he had said impatiently, "Don't you think you can bend enough to call me Mark? I don't bite, even if the State of Hawaii does think I am a—"

"I know," I had cut him off, hating the pain he was suffering but selfishly pleased that the awful thing that had happened to him had brought us together as friends and equals.

We were certainly equals tonight. I explained about falling into the pit in the sand

and then about the trouble with my car, and Mrs. Jeffrey's urging that I stay.

"I don't pretend to understand it, Mark, because I could swear she dislikes me intensely. But she changed and became quite nice."

He took my elbow, saying, "You need something hot inside you. You're freezing. It isn't that cold out. Are you sure you're all right?"

I warmed to his solicitude. He paid no attention when I told him there wasn't anything hot to eat in the house. He took up the lamp, still holding my arm with his free hand, and we went through the house to the kitchen. It was amazing how much less sinister this bleak old hall looked when I saw it in the company of Mark Thursten. I thought of asking him about his locked study, and any number of bothersome happenings of the past few hours, but I didn't want to ruin his return to his home by making trouble between him and his in-laws, and I was beginning to believe all my troubles this evening were due to some magic exerted by that dark-eyed phantom on the beach. With, perhaps, a little help from Mrs. Jeffrey.

In the kitchen Mark produced several oil lamps, filled and lighted them, and then set them around the rooms on the lower floor. To me it was all very festive, and I felt I would never forget just how it was now during the minutes since his arrival—the sudden romantic glow of lamps, the mystery of closed doors suddenly less sinister because Mark was here. As I watched, he produced a bottle of brandy from a high cupboard, explaining that the good liquor in the living room portable bar would probably be gone by now. "It always happens when a place is closed for any time."

I didn't care about the quality of the brandy. I was too busy, in my twenty-two-year-old way, staring at his worn brownish tweed jacket, thinking of him with his arms around me, thinking of him kissing me holding me—and then suddenly a mental image of Sybil's lovely self intervened. My dreams fell apart with a thud. I had never seen Mark kiss Sybil, but I was sure she must have been enormously desirable. Her grace and gaiety and breezy assurance had made her seem so, at any rate.

He poured the brandy that looked sometimes purple and sometimes deep gold in the lamplight, apologizing because the electricity wasn't on yet. I assured him I didn't care in the least.

"And I'm not sick, so I suppose I shouldn't be entitled to any brandy, either. At least," I added, grinning suddenly at a memory, "Dad always said that."

"Must you be sick to drink brandy?" he teased me, but in spite of his light tone I thought he seemed troubled by me, or by something about me. He was looking at me in a very odd way, intent and thoughtful, until I wondered if he was really thinking about me at all. Maybe he was still thinking about his dead wife and that sunny winter day when he came back from Honolulu and the little celebration of my birthday, only to meet the combined accusations of his little daughter and his two in-laws, Carol and Mrs. Jeffrey.

It had always puzzled me that thirteen-year-old Bobbie should stick to her story of the quarrel between her father and mother. In itself, a quarrel between them was not startling. The serious Mark and lighthearted Sybil had occasionally had words even in the presence of the office staff. Or, to be exact, Sybil had words. She called Mark jealous when he objected to her popularity with other men. But none of us had ever heard the shocking thing Bobbie testified to at the trial: "Mommy was in the lanai and I heard her say she was going to leave Daddy if he made trouble for her. And I heard Daddy say she couldn't take me if she did leave him. That was when Mommy said—he wasn't my father."

As even the prosecution agreed, after that there was silence. Nothing more was heard between them. The angry, shocked Mark drove into town, and as for Sybil, her mother and sister claimed no one saw her again until her body was found by a cleaning girl, sprawled across the tiny coral spit in the sand.

Secretly, I often wondered if there had been

another man in Sybil Thursten's life, and even if he could be Bobbie's father, but Mark quietly forbade any further mention of it when his lawyers hinted at a question about Bobbie's parentage. As a result, there had been no effort to follow this lead. At times during the trial I wondered if Mark's reticence was a mistake. Suppose there had been another man in Sybil's life. Wasn't it at least vaguely conceivable that he might have killed her? I couldn't think of a reason, but then, I wasn't a lawyer.

"You are looking very serious," Mark told me now, crooking his forefinger under my chin. "And I promise not to keep you up much longer, but I want you to know that seeing your friendly little face here tonight—even in this ghostly lamplight—is the nicest thing that's happened to me since—" his voice twisted a bit and I looked away, but he finished on even keel "—well, since the last time I saw your friendly little face."

I winced at the repetition of the phrase. I was sure he had never called Sybil's face "friendly little," but I was grateful for small favors, and to keep him away from grim memories, I said hurriedly, "It was nice that you were able to get here tonight. I know Mrs. Jeffrey will think so too. She said she was afraid. But no more than I was." I remembered in time what we were afraid of, and laughed.

"Well, you know women alone at night in an old—I mean an historic house."

He was looking at me with that piercing blue gaze, as if he could read every thought I ever had.

"What do you mean, you were afraid? Was that why I saw you running around in circles out on the sand half an hour ago? What on earth were you afraid of?"

I laughed self-consciously, trying to avoid any mention of his dead wife.

"It's so silly. I thought I saw someone looking in through the screen at me just before you came." I thought I had found a way out when I hobbled on with what I hoped sounded like a logical question. "Could it have been you?"

But I hadn't fooled him. "Good Lord, I don't go tiptoeing around peering in my own windows at midnight." He took me by the shoulders to make me look into his eyes. "I parked my car in front of that ramshackle garage the boys are throwing together, and just as I started across the beach, I saw some fluttery creature running over the sand. So I came after you."

"Then you didn't see anything else except me?" What on earth *was* that thing I had seen at the window?

This time he did smile. "No ghosts, goblins, or poltergeists. Only my night-blooming secretary. We haven't held a séance here in six months. Come along now and pick out one of the bedrooms. My mother-in-law can play the chaperone if you are concerned. You don't want to spend any more time out on that windy lanai. No wonder you fell into *imus* and ran around chasing ghosts."

I was anxious to please him, but I couldn't help grumbling defensively, "It isn't my fault I fell into the pit. I think that beachcomber put a hex on me. He watched me the whole time. I wouldn't put it past him to have dug the hole for me to fall into."

His hands dropped away from my shoulders. Too late, I knew I had upset him in some way. His face had the stiff, too-contained look it had worn at the trial when he denied that his wife had called their daughter illegitimate. He turned back to the brandy decanter, looked at it as if he had never seen it before, and then set it onto the sink counter with a crash. I jumped at the noise and reached out to catch the bottle but it was safe. He had put his own hand out at the same time, and when it closed over mine I wouldn't for worlds have had it any other way. Unfortunately, I couldn't say the same for Mark. His fingers left mine so quickly you'd have thought he had been burned.

"Who was this fellow you say you saw?" he asked me urgently, his voice tense and angry. "Tell me!"

Five

I was so confused by his abrupt shift in mood that I couldn't think for a few seconds what man he was talking about.

"He was hardly real—" I protested finally, wondering why on earth he was so upset.

"For God's sake, don't tell me about any more phantoms," he cut in brusquely, just as I was about to do that very thing. But he looked so terribly troubled that I forgave him his outburst of temper.

I described the man on the beach, and was relieved when Mark nodded as if he was familiar with my phantom.

"Yes. He is probably a fellow named Bates. Writes trash for any crime rags that will take the stuff. Manning says he's been hanging around here lately looking for material."

Manning was the head of the legal firm that had defended Mark, and his identification of the beachcomber bothered me almost as much as had the thought of the dark-eyed Bates being a phantom. Was the beachcomber really hanging around here in order to write about Sybil Thursten's death? I was familiar enough with crime-exposé magazines to imagine the horrible photos of the family, especially of Mark, that would appear beside some scurrilous story slanted just enough to make Mark sound like a murderer.

I made a face and murmured, "I hope he doesn't hang around too long. He gives me the creeps."

Mark put his arm around me and hugged me reassuringly against that rough jacket of his. "Don't worry. I doubt if he'll be in this vicinity for longer than it takes to meet Carol and my mother-in-law. They aren't much for publicity and scandal, any more than I am."

As we left the kitchen, I stopped thinking about Mark long enough to consider what he was saying. "You mean Miss Jeffrey and her mother won't try to tell him all those lies they told in court?"

He stopped to pinch out the candle in a kitchen lamp. "Carol came by today. She was very sweet. A gentle girl. I feel a little sorry for her. I think what happened in court, about Bobbie, was more of a shock to Carol than—" He broke off. "She believed my little girl's story, and that explains her testimony. But now, she has had second thoughts." He shrugged and sighed tiredly. "Anyway, she will be here with Bobbie tomorrow." He glanced at his wrist. "Today, that is, and I want her to stay for a while. It will help Bobbie, I'm sure, to have Carol and her grandmother near. She didn't want to come unless they did."

I didn't dare to disagree with him, but secretly I had my doubts. Maybe it was just jealousy, but I didn't see how Carol and Mrs. Jeffrey could have changed that quickly, that conveniently, for them to live here close by Mark's daughter. God knows what the Jeffreys had told that child during these past five months while they had had her in their control!

"How about it?" He interrupted my unpleasant thoughts briskly. "Have you seen the guest rooms upstairs? Which will you have?"

"Any one of them except—" I bit that off. No use in mentioning his dead wife's elegant white suite. I had a distinct aversion to it, which had increased when Mrs. Jeffrey, in that very odd way, had tried to persuade me to sleep there.

"Except what?" he asked, smiling faintly.

"I meant, any except yours and Mrs. Jeffrey's."

He accepted this unquestioningly, and we made the rounds of the first floor together while he snuffed out most of the candles. Then we went up to the second floor, and for one ghastly minute I thought he *was* going to offer me Sybil Thursten's white suite. Instead, fortunately, he left me in the room across the hall from her bedroom. I found myself quite comfortable there and I stripped off my clothes at last, washed with the bottled water I found in the little bathroom, and crawled into the modern, comfortable double bed with its cool sheets against my reasonably clean flesh.

I did wonder for a few minutes where Mark was sleeping, but I could not tell where he had gone after he left me.

I dozed off and was awakened only once more that night, about forty minutes after I had gone to bed, when I heard a door open and close nearby. I was sure the sound came from across the hall, but there were no more noises and I went back to sleep, wondering if Mark was spending the night in his dead wife's room. I hoped not. It might be meaningful to him, of course, but to my prejudiced senses, it was only morbid.

I woke up a little after sunrise, a lovely vermillion tropical sunrise, and I remembered immediately that I had to get my car fixed and go back to Honolulu. Automatically, I used the bottled water to wash and scrub myself, but it was not a substitute for a warm bath, and along with my stiff, sore—but improving—leg, I must have been a pretty funny sight when, having put on those torn shorts and the rest of my sandy outfit, I tiptoed out into the hall, battered and bandaged.

Among the three of us, Mrs. Jeffrey, Mark, and me, we must have snapped on every light in the place during the preceding night to see if the electricity had been turned on yet—and now it had been. The hall might conceivably need the electric light, but when I got downstairs, I found the lanai lights were on, both kitchen lights, and even one of the lamps in the big living room. I began to turn them off; then, remembering last night's harrowing visit in the lanai, I decided first to examine that room as well as the area surrounding it outside.

The couch looked raggedly comfortable under the piercing brightness of the sunrise, which caught Beach House aslant, its rays partially interrupted by the low reef east of the building. When I walked outside, I saw that the early sun reflected off the easterly windows made the house look as if it were ablaze, an odd and disquieting idea. I found I had been right last night. There were no signs that the dead face I'd seen peering in at me, directly above my couch, had been anything but a product of my overexercised imagination.

As I walked on I noticed some carpenter's tools, including a low step ladder propped up against the house, partly covered by a tarpaulin. I guessed they were being used by Joe Nakazawa and his friend to build the garage, but it seemed possible that if anyone had wanted to stare in at me, scaring me half to death, that stepladder would have been handy for the purpose. In a way it was reassuring. Ghostly dead women don't need ladders, I reasoned as I came back around the house and went up the stairs again.

Someone was at the lanai door, which opened for me abruptly. I should not have been shaken—but I was—to see Mrs. Jeffrey there, wearing another of those currently fashionable belted creations that was a cross between a hostess gown and a too-long bathrobe. Its length, for it almost covered her shoe tops, along with the high-coiffed gray-white hair, made her look preternaturally tall. I was sure she dressed this way to be startling; she achieved her effect, as far as I was concerned.

"How fortunate you are up, Miss Carter! My son-in-law was just saying he wanted to drive you into the city for your—clothing." She paused just long enough to make me horribly conscious of the leggy mess I must appear to her, and especially to Mark, in my striped pullover and shorts. I'm sure I must have reddened at the reminder, but I came in breezily past her and ostentatiously crossed the living room to turn off the still-burning lamp.

She moved along after me, her eyes noting my every motion, but the minute we heard Mark's step in the hall, she changed. The aloofness and frigid manner remained, but there was a gracious Grand Lady quality that overlaid the naked hate she sometimes showed me. I had a feeling she didn't like her son-in-law any better than she liked me, though she was too good a tactician to show it now. For some reason—possibly not for Bobbie alone—she wanted to remain in this house where her daughter had died, and she wanted to put a gloss of goodwill on her relationship with the house's owner.

Mark was in the hall doorway with a beat-up jacket over his broad shoulders. He wore slacks and a dark blue shirt that wasn't quite an *aloha* shirt. I was relieved to see how cheerful he looked. But it turned out that I was providing some of his cheer, and in the most humiliating way. He looked me up and down, smiled and said, "Come along, litle girl. We'll have breakfast in the village. I want to get to the office in time for the mainland flights." All our mainland mail was naturally by air, and flight times were important in the Islands.

As I hurried to obey, he took my hand and swung it the way he might have swung his daughter's hand, remarking while we went out through the lanai, "You do look exactly like a little girl, you know, in that ridiculous outfit."

We passed the place where his wife had died, and though he didn't seem to notice it, I was all the more aware of it because his remark to me pointed up the enormous difference between Sybil and me. Every time I looked down at my sandy clothes and expanse of bare skin, I could have crawled away out of sight, but I was so busy trying to keep up with Mark's long strides that I soon forgot my humiliation.

Things didn't get any better during the rest of the morning, though. Mark liked to eat breakfast in silence, and this reminded me that he was my employer. I hardly said more than "Please pass the sugar," and drank my papaya juice and the delicious Kona Coffee in what I hoped was an inscrutable silence.

We were leaving the little restaurant when a young man, about to enter, stopped to hold the door open for us. It was a shock to me when I came within inches of the dark eyes, the chiseled features, and the smile that belonged to my phantom beachcomber. The striking good looks of the creature only made him seem more malevolent by contrast, when I recalled that he went around writing scurrilous stories concerning famous crimes. I pretended not to know him, but he had the nerve to greet me like an old friend.

"Good morning. Feeling better, I hope. No bad effects?"

Mark glanced from me to the dark-eyed man, plainly puzzled. I tried to explain the situation to Mark while I answered the beachcomber-author.

"I recovered nicely. A silly accident, wasn't it?"

Mark looked as if he hadn't heard me correctly, but the nasty Bates merely shrugged. Didn't he have any other clothes except that sinister black "uniform" of his?

"Well," he said in a provoking tone, "everything can't always go as we plan it." And as I turned away angrily, taking Mark's arm, which the fellow obviously noticed, he had the nerve to add his black joke: "Better luck next time." He put up three fingers to his unruly black hair, saluted us in his sardonic way, and went on into the restaurant.

"What the devil was that all about?" Mark asked as we got into his car.

"Isn't that the man named Bates, who's looking for scandals to write about?"

Frowning, Mark leaned out of the the car to stare at the restaurant door, which was still swinging. "So that's what he looks like! Hardly more than a boy. Is he a hippie or something?"

I laughed. "I don't think so. He just has a weird sense of humor."

We hardly said anything more all the way across the island. I am talkative by nature and I felt hurt and worried, thinking I had somehow offended him, that I had been too friendly, had overstepped the bounds of our relationship. But when we drove out Kalakaua Avenue to my apartment four blocks from Waikiki Beach he let me out in what was, for my employer, a thorough good humor.

"Pack for a month or so. Take all the little odds and ends you women find so necessary. I'm going to handle my work from Beach House for a few weeks. And you can be of more use there than downtown. Don't worry. You will be properly chaperoned."

A month or so! I was so surprised I questioned his decision, which I wouldn't have dreamed of doing in other circumstances. "But Mrs. Jeffrey says she and Carol will be staying. And of course, your daughter. Won't it be hard to work with all those females around you?"

He waved away my objection. "There may be things to find out among those females. Or that pretty boyfriend of yours with the penchant for beaches at night."

I immediately guessed what he was up to. If he suspected that Sybil actually had been murdered, it seemed logical that one of his in-laws, or possibly my "boyfriend with the penchant for beaches" might be guilty. It was a terrible possibility and it gave me chills to think of it. Besides, in all likelihood Mrs. Thursten had died accidentally. That was the assumption of the jury when Mark was found not guilty. But I could imagine his interest in investigating, if, as I suspected, Mark believed his wife really had been murdered.

I said, "Yes. I'll go and change and pack. Where should I meet you?"

"Here, of course," he said impatiently. "Can

you be ready in an hour? I'll go to the office now. Oh—and, Livia—bring shorthand note-books. You can use Sybil's electric typewriter."

I gave him a big smile and rushed into my apartment building as he drove away. At once I started reviewing the time we had spent to-gether. There had been moments when he seemed to forget I was his secretary and treated me like a friend, or even like his daughter. It was at least a step closer than the cold click-click relationship we had known for the past year.

Give him time, the mature part of my judg-ment told me. . . . It's only six months since Sybil died. Gay, laughing, irresponsible Sybil Thursten, who really had done me no harm except to be the wife of the only man I wanted. I was sure she could have had any man she'd set her sights on. If she had known that good-looking beachcomber who wrote trashy stories, surely he would have been attracted to her.

In fact . . . perhaps she had known him.

All the while I showered, dressed, and packed for my stay at Beach House, I consid-ered the young man named Bates, his apparent hatred of me and perhaps of Mark too and his British accent, so like that of Mrs. Jeffrey—which seemed too much of a coincidence. There might very well have been something between Bates and Sybil Thursten. There was that dreadful statement Mark's little girl had made on the witness stand: "Mummy said he wasn't my father."

Mark believed it was a lie, a cruel lie that someone had told Bobbie to say on the witness stand.

Could Bates be that father? Most unlikely. He was probably too young to have been mixed up with Sybil and far too young to be Bobbie Thursten's father. Still, there seemed to be endless secrets surrounding Sybil's death. And Bates might even be older than he looked. It still seemed most unlikely, though, that Bobbie Thursten was anyone's child but Mark's. She had Mark's disposition—his long silences—and his lean, sinewy build. But she also had dark hair and eyes, a trifle like Bates, now that I thought of it.

What on earth *was* Bates' interest in the inhabitants of Beach House—if it went beyond an unsavory story? I wondered again if he had covered over that *imu* so I would fall into it. Or *was* it I who was meant to fall into it? This idea made me stop in the middle of packing while I considered the alternatives. But it was too much for me. I ended by deciding I had been right in the first place. Sybil Thursten had died by accident. The dark-eyed beachcomber was hanging around purely to get a story.

I got packed so quickly I had to wait ten minutes or so before Mark was due to drive by and pick me up. While I waited, nervously going back and forth to my third-floor windows to watch the street beyond the apartment court-yard, I was interested to see a taxi drive up and a young woman get out. She looked familiar, and when she was followed by a tall young teen-ager with her straight dark hair dangling below her shoulders, I knew Mark's daughter, Bobbie, had been brought to my place by his sister-in-law, Carol Jeffrey. Several suitcases were unloaded by the time I got downstairs to welcome the two girls.

I decided Mark must have asked them to meet me here so he could pick us up together. When I met Carol, it turned out that I'd guessed right. I was relieved to find her outwardly friendly; anything else would have made our situation at Beach House impossible. Carol was about twenty-five or so, and had good features that she didn't utilize to their best advantage. Her big hazel eyes looked sincere enough to make their earlier dislike of me most poignant; she seemed much easier to like than her fascinating sister, Sybil. Carol wore her dusky blonde hair lank behind her ears, which did nothing for a face slightly too wide across the cheekbones. Sybil, with many of the same characteristics, had used every artifice to play up her best features, for which I would have admired her if I hadn't felt that burning young jealousy. I wondered suddenly if Carol had ever been equally jealous of her stunning sister.

Carol hesitated as we met in the little courtyard under the line of gaunt and naked palms. I was so anxious to be friendly I almost overdid it, but luckily she reciprocated, giving me her slow, shy smile; quite different from the cold-eyed scowl I got from young Bobbie.

"Are we all going out together? That's nice," I said inanely. Carol had started to shake hands, then withdrew hers, seeing that I hadn't expected it, which left me in the position of dangling a belated, empty hand. I started to move their baggage to one side of the courtyard and she helped me. I looked at Bobbie, expecting her to join in. She had, in my brief experience, formerly possessed very good manners, but something had certainly happened to those manners now. She seemed keyed up and nervous, and there was no mistaking the unadulterated animosity in her eyes when she looked at me.

I said, "How do you like your school, Bobbie?"

She shrugged. "I don't have to go back till fall. They let me off this term on account of Mother being murdered and all."

Carol glanced quickly at me, then away. "Bobbie . . ." she reminded the girl in an anxious way, "we aren't going to talk about that. Remember?"

"Sure," Bobbie came back coldly. "You said we could think about it all we want, but we mustn't say anything. Okay, I won't." She picked up a long, wide, flat package from among the suitcases and hugged it to her thin, undeveloped young breast. "This will settle things."

Carol and I, who were moving a big plaid pullman case together, stopped and looked at her. The girl's attitude was odd, as if she had her mind on faraway things and was hardly aware of us. I whispered, "Is she all right?"

"Certainly," Carol said, an indignant edge to her voice. "You can't blame her for feeling this way. In view of what's happened. Shall we go up and get your things?"

I felt properly snubbed, but told her she needn't come, and went back by myself. The maintenance man carried my suitcase and makeup kit down, and I took various secretarial materials in a big attaché case.

When my baggage had been added to Bobbie's and Carol's, the latter for the first time showed a little of the malign quality that Mrs. Jeffrey carried around with her like a hair shirt.

"You always manage to get men to do your . . . work, don't you?"

I was sure she had started to say my "dirty work," but I pretended not to notice. I said to Bobbie, coolly but politely, "Shall we put your package with the rest?"

79

The girl looked down at it but only hugged it tighter and shook her head. I saw Carol give me a side-glance that made me more uneasy than Bobbie's outright hostility.

"What's in it?" I asked more sharply than I meant to.

"A Ouija board. Aunt Carol and Grandma say we are going to call up my mother's spirit on it." Seeing my stupefaction, Bobbie went on in a perfectly pleasant, normal thirteen-year-old voice, "If you and *he* didn't do it together and make up an alibi, then you won't be frightened to have Mother come back, will you?"

The fact that I was innocent did not prevent me from being every bit as taken aback as she had intended me to be.

Six

Carol saved me from a disastrous betrayal of my distress. "Really, Bobbie, you know you shouldn't talk like that. It's only a game. Just a board that depends on vibrations and perspiration in your hands or something."

I managed a weak smile. "I know it's only a game, but I remember an old lady when I was a girl. She had the most amazing results with Ouija boards. I used to run and hide when she came visiting us."

"You mustn't run and hide this time," young Bobbie told me with the persistence of childhood. "It won't be any fun if you don't play, too." She stopped at a quick warning look from Carol, then went on, speaking very fast. "I didn't mean to scare you, Livia. We need you to play. Otherwise it won't work."

I was greatly relieved to see Mark's car drive up just then, and Carol and I both changed the subject and greeted Mark. It was a piercingly clear day, and the lush, romantic odor of the humble plumeria filled the air. But my thoughts were not romantic. I kept wondering about the Ouija board Bobbie hugged so tenaciously, and wondering, too, about Carol's feelings toward Mark. Whatever her suspicions of him, she hadn't managed to kill the infatuation I was sure she felt for him. I could tell it by her tremulous manner with him. It was so very like my own.

Mark had gone up to Bobbie first to embrace her, but she squealed, "Ouch! You'll break my game board!" and his hands slowly moved away from her. It made me almost ill to see all the gaiety and lightness in his face die out and that somber look come back. But he would not force the issue. He began calmly to load the trunk of the car. I noticed that Carol was watching him much as I was, hoping his depression would pass. She looked flushed and sympathetic. Whether Bobbie's behavior had been prompted by Carol or not, I felt that Carol's feelings for her brother-in-law were as genuine as mine, and that she too suffered from her young niece's cold-blooded attitude toward him.

When we drove back across the island, it was a relief to me to have Bobbie share the front seat with Mark while Carol and I sat in the back. I kept hoping Bobbie would thaw toward her father.

As for Carol, it took some time for her to

show signs of her ambivalent feelings toward her brother-in-law, but, by the time we passed Wahiawa she was whispering to me, "I'm sure Bobbie will feel different after a little while with her father. It's been such a long time. And when you consider what she knows!"

I nodded, hoping she was right about Bobbie's mood, and because I couldn't resist the question any longer, I whispered, "Was that her idea about the Ouija board?"

Carol studied her short, ragged fingernails. She said finally, "In a way. She read about it. And Mother asked her to get one."

"You mean your mother believes in things like that?"

I did not add that I myself was fascinated by such things. I made up my mind on the spot that I wasn't going to be taken in by this one. Angry and resentful over what I now thought of as the Jeffreys' tricks, tricks directed not only against me but very likely against Mark as well, I decided to spike Carol's little guns if, in fact, she and her mother were planning something in the way of apparitions for some peculiar satisfaction of their own.

"It's a waste of time, you know, using Ouija boards and séances to bring someone back. I saw one of those tricks last night. Almost, but not quite, convincing."

I watched her for some reaction and it was unquestionably there; she stiffened, started to

speak, then wet her lips and whispered broken-
ly, "No—trick. Have you no shame at all? After
what you did?"

I gave up. She was incredible. She must
think I had split myself in two the day of Sybil's death, with half of me in Honolulu and
the other half at Beach House shoving her sister off the steps ten minutes after she'd had a
violent quarrel with Mark. If, as it now seemed
likely, the Jeffreys thought I was either a mur-
deress or the accomplice to Mark's crime, I
could hardly be any more safe at Beach House
now than I was last night when I had felt so
stifled by the ambiguous enmity of Mrs. Jeffrey.
Today there were apparently two other enemies. One was open and aboveboard; that was
thirteen-year-old Bobbie. And the other, fully
as sinister as her mother, I now thought, was
Carol Jeffrey, whose sweet smile and sad eyes
would no longer fool me.

Carol now leaned forward to tell Mark that
her little car was being repaired, and that a
friend was going to deliver it at Beach House
for her later in the day. After that we drove in
silence; then I was relieved to hear Bobbie in
the front seat begin to chatter to her father,
who had finally got her onto a subject she
couldn't resist.

"Can we really have a luau ourselves? Can I
run it? Not the pig. That's too hard. But wien-
ies and steaks and all?"

"Certainly. Maybe a roast of pork too. And *poi* and *lomilomi* salmon and coconut pudding and all the rest."

"Mother would have liked that. She always liked parties," Bobbie remarked matter-of-factly, without any self-consciousness.

At mention of his wife, Mark's voice took on the old, deep, throbbing note I would have given anything to arouse in him.

"Yes. She would have liked it. Your mother always liked the beach."

Bobbie murmured in wonder, "On the roughest days, even. I remember she used to walk all alone for ages. . . . I wonder if she ever met anyone."

Carol and I stiffened and looked at each other in mutual anxiety, but neither Bobbie nor Mark seemed to have read any significance into her remark.

"All alone. Your mother liked to be alone." Was there any meaning to his hesitation, I wondered, before he resumed, "Who would she meet? There isn't another house on the shore until beyond Makai Point."

"That's right. I forgot." The girl settled down in her seat, the little spurt of affection and interest gone.

I sat there resenting Carol and Mrs. Jeffrey for planting horrible suspicions in Bobbie's mind. Not once during the conversation had she called Mark "Father." I laid the responsibility for this to the Jeffreys, who must have primed her to tell the police that awful lie and then to repeat it on the witness stand. If, of course, it really *was* a lie. It was not until she talked to the police that Bobbie had mentioned the deadly fact that her mother had denied that Mark was her father. Many people wondered how much the Jeffreys had to do with this appalling statement. I didn't know Sybil Thursten well enough to be certain that she hadn't betrayed Mark. And if this was the case, I couldn't blame Mark for swearing on the witness stand that she had not said it. It had to be a lie, and a cruel one, for Sybil Thursten, thirteen years after Bobbie's birth, to spread such a story of Bobbie's illegitimacy.

I knew by this time that Bobbie would make no further flat declaration that she believed a crime had been committed, but the child was far from blind. She would, somehow, get her point over. I only hoped she would learn the truth, and free Mark and me from her suspicions. The enormous amount of hypocrisy that I had seen applied against my employer during the trial, and again now when the trial was over, made me all the more anxious to assure myself that Bobbie saw and heard the real truth, whatever it might be. To me, at my age, it was all quite simple. Truth and falsehood in life were as simple as explaining to Bobbie that her mother was not an adulteress. In Bobbie's present mood, it seemed clear to me that it would be easier and less painful to demonstrate at Beach House how life might take on new meaning, new warmth, if only she could retain a fairly adult calm and self-confidence. She would also need an open mind, and helping her to attain one appeared to be the first objective for Mark and those who cared for him.

It was still sunny, but the air was cool and nippy by the time we reached the windward coast and Beach House. I was relieved to see that the help had arrived and supplies were being unloaded. The little Japanese cook superintended the transfer of endless frozen items into the big freezer in the rear entry hall. Numerous brown bags of fresh vegetables and groceries were stacked around the kitchen, as I could see when we passed the open windows on our way to the front entrance.

Mark put one arm around his daughter as they walked up the steps and then stood aside for us to enter the lanai, but before we could move further, Bobbie stopped abruptly and gestured toward the stair beneath her feet.

"Here's where Mother was when it happened. The argument, I mean. And you—" she nodded at Mark, her lank straight hair swinging, "—you were right where you are now. And you quarreled. And Mother said you weren't my father. Of course, that may not have been just before Mother died. Even I know that."

I saw Mark's faint movement, like a shudder, but he was gentle with her. "That's not true, Bobbie. You must have misunderstood her. Remember, you didn't see us when we were . . . talking. Your mother talks—talked rapidly, and the wind was blowing. You weren't even outside at the time."

"I was on the upstairs lanai overhead. The lanai outside Mother's bedroom. . . . Let's go in now, shall we?"

I looked coldly at Carol, trying in that one intent look to tell her that I suspected where young Bobbie had really gotten this dreadful idea about her illegitimacy. Carol ducked her head and hurried in while Mark held the door open. She looked shamefaced, probably because she shared my feeling for Mark. The one thing I had always suspected since the day I was chosen as his secretary instead of Carol was that we had in common a violent crush on "the boss."

"Mama?" she called, hurrying through the house. "We're here. Bobbie and I are here. Where are you?"

In spite of the servants in the back of the house, the sound of her voice echoed through deserted rooms. She peered into rooms on the east side of the house, which had by this hour lost the now westerly sunshine, and I was sure

Carol didn't like those dark rooms any better than I did. She saw me watching her, and rolled her eyes as though she and I shared a secret about the grim Victorian nooks and crannies.

Mark spoke to her suddenly and she jumped. Evidently she hadn't realized he was so near.

"If you are uncomfortable here, Carol, we'll make some other arrangements."

"No, no," she said hurriedly. "I love it here. It's so quaint."

"It's all of that," I thought, but what really puzzled me was her extraordinary anxiety to remain in a place she clearly hated and found repugnant, in spite of Bobbie. What were the Jeffreys really up to at Beach House?

I was still wondering about this when young Joe Nakazawa came in with my suitcases, looking all around as if he expected ghosts to creep out of the woodwork.

"I thought you wouldn't set foot in this house," I reminded him.

He grinned. "I got my arm twisted. Financially speaking. Anyway, you won't catch me here after dark." He appeared to think this over and added with a glance up the stairs, "Unless there's a party going on. I spent a whole evening once dancing with Mrs. Thursten. A great girl, that one. You'd have thought she was—well—younger than me. Where to, lady?"

I told him, "Upstairs and turn to the left,"

and was about to follow him when Mark touched me on the hand.

"Livia, I'd like to talk to you."

I followed him and found myself waiting outside his locked study while he looked through his haphazard collection of keys. "I had the impression none of these doors were locked when I left. Did you lock this room to keep prowlers out?"

I said I hadn't. He opened the door and let me in. I expected to get a slap of dust and stale air, but the small study was surprisingly pleasant, clean and dust-free. I didn't know whether he'd noticed this, and if he had, whether it seemed as strange to him as it did to me. Tentatively, I suggested, "Now that it's open, I'll clean it up and get your papers ready. . . ."

He was studying his desk, which seemed, to me at least, very much as he had left it, with his charts and folders and scrap paper all where they should be. But when he opened the desk drawers, he frowned.

"I don't remember leaving things in this mess, do you?" I looked in. Charts, reports, his personal writing paper, even some ball-point pens, were all crammed into the center drawer as though they had been brushed off the desk top in a great hurry.

"No. I'm sure it wasn't." Feeling guilty, although I would never have left his things in this condition, I said nervously, "You know I never leave your desk disordered downtown."

He looked over at me and smiled, one of those rare, warming glances I treasured and for which I sometimes waited, it seemed, days.

"You take very good care of me. None better. I know that. . . . And I know I was pretty upset the day I left here. It is possible, of course, that one of the servants simply dusted the desk and emptied extras into this drawer."

"But they shouldn't have! I mean, I came and got your things and brought them to the—to you in town. But I didn't do this. As a matter of fact, I distinctly remember putting the old reports in your Quarterly Orient folder."

I watched him drum lean, strong fingers on the desk top, and I wondered who had gone through his papers—and why. Mrs. Jeffrey had been in the house alone, but that she should have an interest in his business papers seemed odd. I could picture her searching through her dead daughter's suite for something that might, if discovered, compromise Sybil's reputation. But this hurried ransacking of Mark's desk drawers—what sort of evidence was someone looking for here?

He was very much troubled in spite of his gentle treatment of me, and I didn't want to upset him further. It may have been that this curious little mystery had come too close on his return home, his first return since Sybil's death. I wondered if he was thinking of her now. I pretended to examine the window locks. They were flimsy enough. The old-fashioned shutters were merely decorative, and fastened back against the house. There were maroon drapes at the windows but they were parted a few inches. . . . There was enough light to illuminate a portion of the room in the daytime, though hardly at night.

Over beneath the book shelves I saw something I knew shouldn't normally be found here. I stooped to pick up the tiny battery and examined it in my palm.

"What have you got there?"

"A flashlight battery, I think. The kind they use in little key lights. Or maybe it's from a very small transistor radio," I added doubtfully.

He took it from me, weighing it in his hand as he glanced around the floor where I had found it. "I imagine it rolled over here against the book shelf, and whoever lost it couldn't find it in the dark."

There was a small sound in the doorway, a kind of sigh, and we looked around together. I felt as nervous as if I'd been caught in a crime. Perhaps this reaction was simply the reflection of the look I read in Bobbie Thursten's eyes.

"What are you doing?" she asked us accusingly.

Mark very properly dismissed me, the way

employers do. "Excuse me. We'll talk about this later."

He dropped the battery into the pocket of his jacket and crossed the room to Bobbie; I could see the effort it was for him to play the lighthearted parent when he was so evidently hurt by her mistrust and by the way she persistently avoided calling him "Father."

"Bobbie, shall we go up and see how comfortable you are in your rooms? How do you like them? You're too big now for that nursery affair you used to have."

"I want to be next to Carol," she complained flatly as they walked to the stairs.

Feeling let down and unable to blame anyone for it, I was grateful to the ever-peppy Joe Nakazawa, who was in the kitchen eating a stalk of raw celery he'd gotten from the genial little cook, Mrs. Tomei. They seemed the best of friends, and it occurred to me that between Mrs. Tomei and Joe's mother, who owned the store in the village, they probably knew more than I did about affairs in the household.

Joe called to me. "Any other little chores, lady? I'm not staying after dark."

"Joe, you are very silly boy," said Mrs. Tomei, waving a gleaming bone chopper at him. "It is bad boys like you make these stories about Beach House. Not a word is true," she assured me. "My family and I have been friends with the Thurstens since the old captain brought my grandfather from Nagasaki to the Islands. The captain and my grandfather were both poor. But the Islands were good to them."

"Good to the Thurstens, anyway," Joe put in. " 'Kay, now. Got to get home and cram for that cotton-picking Biology final tomorrow."

We waved good-bye to him and watched him loping off down the dusty road toward the village. I offered to help Mrs. Tomei put away the vegetables and canned goods on shelves too high for her to reach, and I remarked on how much I appreciated good food, especially after last night's meal of whatever a can opener would furnish unheated. I was still stacking away groceries, and Mrs. Tomei was marinating succulent strips of tender steak for one of her Japanese recipes, when Bobbie's voice reached us clearly from the top of the back stairs. She sounded like a child in a temper tantrum, younger than her years.

"I just won't! You can't make me sleep next to that—that awful Carter woman! I want the room next to Carol, I tell you!"

"Don't, dear. Please be good now. You promised. It's only for a little while. Then the bad woman will be gone."

I didn't at first recognize the quiet, soothing voice, but it evidently calmed Bobbie down, because we heard no more. The embarrassed Mrs. Tomei tried to explain to me. "They have always been friends. Miss Jeffrey was often the baby-sitter, you know, when Mrs. Thursten went into town."

"Did she go into town often?" I despised my own suspicious curiosity, but I couldn't resist the question. Besides, I wanted to stop wondering what Carol Jeffrey had meant when she soothed her niece with the promise that "the bad woman will be gone."

"Only toward the last. Then she went often. Or she walked along the shore for hours at a time."

"At least she didn't fall into that pit out there first," I said grumpily, staring at the long, lonely beach.

The little cook came up behind me and looked out over my shoulder. "Very strange," she murmured, shaking her head. "That is a poor place for the *imu*. It was never there in Mrs. Thursten's time."

"What!"

"It is so. Joe and I were saying an hour ago that the *imu* was not there last Sunday when Joe and my daughter and some friends went surf casting."

I decided I would ask Joe Nakazawa if he had seen people on the beach, maybe digging the pit. Joe and his college friend had been working on the garage for days. They might have seen something. If there was anything to see.

"Ah," said Mrs. Tomei with interest, pointing down the beach. "There is the handsome malihini. My daughter and her friends find him so very—how is it they talk? Living dolls. That is what they say. A living doll. Very odd, don't you think? But I will not let my girl go into town with him."

"Good Lord! I should hope not. It's *him*!"

"You find him a living doll too, Miss Carter?"

"Not for me, thank you!"

The dark-eyed beachcomber had appeared from nowhere and stood now on the sand. In the afternoon light his slight figure cast an elongated shadow toward us.

Mrs. Tomei said wisely, "There are times he waits like death. All in black. You will see. Like death, he is."

"Waits? What for?"

She turned from the window and went back to her work.

"But for someone in Beach House. It is certain."

Seven

I felt strongly tempted to go out and beard the lion, challenge this fellow and find out who his accomplice or whatever in the house might be, but an unusual attack of common sense stopped me just in time. As long as Mark Thursten was in the house, this was his business and I shouldn't interfere. At best I was only here on sufferance, and the Jeffreys would dislike me worse than ever. Mark himself might consider me a busybody. I did wish, though, that I knew which member of the household this "death image" was concerned with.

On a sudden thought I excused myself to Mrs. Tomei. "I've got to go up and unpack." As I was starting toward the stairs at the front of the house, she suggested,

"The back stairs are quicker, miss."

I grinned and reminded her in a half whisper, "But that man's friend seems to be in the front of the house."

"So." She nodded approvingly, her dark eyes understanding and very serious.

I moved through the now shadowy house toward the front stairs and went up, trying not to make a sound. Unfortunately, all the bedroom doors upstairs were closed. I could hear a shower running somewhere, and in another room the click-click of clothes hangers being pushed along a closet rod. Everything seemed normal.

In my own room opposite the white suite I began to unpack, but my thoughts were still on recent events, especially someone's curious relationship with that dark-eyed death image. It occurred to me suddenly that although everyone in the house seemed to be busy unpacking, showering, and settling in, one member of our lively little group need not unpack at all. When I'd met Mrs. Jeffrey yesterday, she had been very much at home. Also, remembering Mrs. Tomei's remarks about the newness of that *imu* out on the beach, I thought that this too, according to the evidence, could be the work of someone following Mrs. Jeffrey's instructions. She had been the only one here at the time, and Bates, our Friendly Neighborhood Beachcomber, could be working for her.

I went ahead with my own chores, putting away my things, but I did shiver a bit occasionally. I wasn't used to antagonism. It was a feeling that was always with me here, and I didn't like it. I had barely finished when the door opened between my bathroom and the dressing room beyond, which was not mine. I had thought the doors were locked between. But there seemed to be no keys about. I didn't like the notion of people walking in and out of my bedroom any time they wanted to, from either of two directions, but I had some slight hope of better relations when I saw that my visitor was young Bobbie, acting quite civil, even a bit sheepish.

"Hi. Carol says I should apologize. On account of—" She stopped. Her eyes took on the direct, bold look I recognized as like her father's when he was most alone, most in need of friendship and understanding.

"Me too," I said quickly, smiling. "Let's say one cancels out the other. Are you my neighbor?"

"No! That is—" She shrugged, and scuffed her shoe over the rug beside my bed. "I guess so." She looked at me uneasily. "He promised we can have a fire in the living room fireplace if I get some driftwood. You can help me if you want."

She had no sooner finished making this offer when she turned away as if she expected a rebuff. She shrugged. "Not that it matters."

I had already changed for dinner, into one of my most flattering new full-skirted sundresses with a flamboyant Hawaiian pattern that was happy if not subtle, but I couldn't afford to turn down the only olive branch that had been offered me, and I said hurriedly, "I'd love to help. Really."

She stopped and stared at me, scowling as if she was puzzling out something. "You mean it?"

"Just give me a sec. I'll find a sweater. Okay. Let's go."

She didn't wait for me or take my arm or even suggest that we were together, but as she stalked out the doorway ahead of me into the hall, she tossed her dark mane over her shoulder and looked back at me to see if I was coming. In the hall she glanced over at her mother's closed door, and I wondered what she was thinking about Sybil Thursten's suite. Did she find it as strangely evocative of its original inhabitant as I did?

Bobbie's tanned features seemed more strained and tense as we went down the stairs, but that was not surprising. I had never doubted her deep devotion to her lighthearted mother. I often suspected that both Bobbie and Mark, with their innate seriousness, were all the more drawn to Sybil because she was so different. It was at such moments that I felt discouraged about my own power ever to arouse in Mark the kind of feelings he'd had for Sybil. I was certainly a cheerful, extroverted type, but I did not possess the almost wild gaiety that had marked Sybil Thursten.

It was dusk now, and electric lights were on in every room, making the house appear much more friendly, at least while one remained near the various lamps. In the dark stretches between, with their pervasive scent of weathered and dusty wood, it might as well have been last night with the candlelight. The feeling, to me, at least, had not much improved. However, I was counting on one step forward if I could possibly win over Bobbie Thursten. I still wasn't sure of her, and I even looked around, as we left the house by the lanai steps, to be sure she didn't lead me into some unpleasant surprise like another hastily dug pit.

Even the afterglow of sunset was gone now, and our beach world looked indistinct, all the outlines blurred. It gave me a slightly dazed feeling, as if I needed glasses to bring the dulled edges of things into clear focus. I couldn't see anyone else on the beach and wondered where Bates had disappeared to. I didn't want him slipping up on me in his graceful feline way. Bobbie began to dart around the beach, collecting twisted, gnarled gray driftwood, hardly enough to make kindling, and I followed her lead, but I was still watchful, not entirely trusting her.

After a few minutes she came past me to lay her small firewood collection beside the steps.

Empty-handed, she stood there facing me, but staring over my shoulder in an unnerving way. It took all my willpower to refrain from doing the same thing.

"What is it?" I asked, far more calmly than I felt in that gray and shapeless dusk.

She had an intent, serious expression, which almost made me believe she was sincere. "I was just thinking. This time of day I always think of . . . dead things. You can see almost anything along the beach about this hour. Just before it gets really dark, you know."

"Werewolves? Vampires?" I asked brightly, and I was surprised to see her frown, as if I had destroyed her mood by a stupid joke.

"No. Not things like that. Don't be silly. I mean—if Mother ever came back, she'd come at this hour, I bet. At least," she added, "this is when they talked about it. They said it might be a mistake to have séances in the middle of the evening. They should be at the—what they called 'the break of time' between day and night. Or between night and morning. . . . Does that make sense to you?"

I found myself swallowing nervously, and could only shrug.

"Anyway, Mother said if she came back, she'd at least have some point to it, not just come back for no reason."

I held very tight rein on my nerves to keep

from shivering. "Why do you think she would come back at all?"

This time she avoided my eyes, an unusual thing in the direct and brutally frank Bobbie Thursten.

"To tell how she really died. That's why. So I can get vengeance."

It was a ridiculous word on the lips of a thirteen-year-old girl, and yet, like some other ridiculous-sounding things, it had a kind of bloodcurdling reality because she was almost young enough and unsophisticated enough to mean it.

"You will find, Bobbie, that there isn't anything in the whole world as unsatisfying as revenge. It will sicken you." I watched her without seeming to as I went on slowly, with every ounce of sincerity of which I was capable. "Stop and think of the person who told you to hate your father, or to hate me. Don't you see how that person has changed, corroded, become something mean and hard and inhuman, since she—or he—set you onto this bitterness?"

I knew I had struck the right note. Whoever was instructing her in this rottenness must have flashed before her mind's eye now, and Bobbie saw exactly what I described ... no longer the person she had loved and trusted but someone twisted with hate until even the old, living relationship had gone. Bobbie moved away from me, her eyes slowly seeking the driftwood at our feet, but I was rewarded and intensely relieved when she said vaguely,

"I don't know. . . . *I just don't know.*"

It was a step in the right direction. I was grateful for even this much. If I could only get her to turn back to her father, the greatest crisis would be over.

Because I was alert, I saw Bates before she appeared to. He was suddenly at the northeast corner of the house, as if he had strolled down from the unfinished garage, although I had not seen him a few minutes earlier. It was difficult to make out his expression in the gathering twilight, but I reached down to pick up an interesting serpentlike piece of wood and let my gaze wander slightly to the right, where I could clearly see those brilliant, satirical eyes of his as I straightened up again. Surprisingly enough, I thought he looked amused. It might, of course, be that cynical and cutting amusement that had previously revealed dislike of me. I had half an idea of walking up to him and demanding to know what he wanted. While I was still wrestling indignantly with this notion, Bobbie saw him, whether for the first time or not I couldn't tell. She waved to him.

"I want you to meet a real groovy guy. You'll adore him, Livia. He's dying to know you."

I doubted that, but obediently went with her, very curious to see why these two had arranged this meeting. I was sure it had been planned.

The man Bates had not moved from the spot where I first saw him. I tried to find in his face some softening of that satirical look as he spoke to Bobbie, but if he had any warmth or interest in her he certainly did not show it. He made a big and rather obvious play for me then, which I found disconcerting. I was far from unaware of his curious charm.

"Thanks, Bobbie," he said. "I knew I could count on you." And he turned to me with such a coaxing look I found it terribly hard to remain suspicious. "I'm sorry about last night, Miss Carter. I really am. But I was thinking about Bobbie's mother. She was very good to me. And somehow, I expected you to be quite different."

"I know," I said coolly, careful not to look at Bobbie. "Everybody seems to think I'm some kind of monster, just because I told the truth at the trial. Mrs. Thursten undoubtedly died of an accidental fall. I don't know why a few people refuse to believe that."

Bobbie cleared her throat and I thought she would argue this, but she didn't. She pretended to be busy picking up bits of wood, an unconvincing performance. There wasn't that much wood around and it was getting quite dark. I could hardly see her, though I was very conscious of the dark-eyed Bates looking me over, agreeing courteously that I was right: suspicions were useless.

"And did Bobbie tell you that I scribble?" he asked me, as I was about to head for the steps. Although he didn't lay a hand on me, he was obviously trying to prevent me from going indoors.

"You write true crime stories. But there was no crime here," I reminded him. "May I give you a piece of advice?"

He looked awfully surprised, and his shadowy face lighted with amusement. "Go ahead. I may even take it. . . . Bobbie! She's not only pretty but bright. She is going to advise us."

I glanced over my shoulder, but Bobbie had gone up the steps, and was opening the lanai door; I doubted if she'd even heard him. I certainly had no intention of staying out here alone with him for long. Even now, I was far from certain that he wasn't up to something. I said icily, "My advice is—tell the story about how you and the others forced a girl to lie about her father under oath, how you persuaded her, you and her other friends, of all kinds of vile insinuations. And my best advice of all is for you to stay as far away from Beach House as possible."

This time, as I saw the lanai door open again, and assumed Bobbie was waiting for me, I tried to get past him. I thought for a shaky second or two that he was going to stop me, but he merely said quietly, "I'm sorry to disappoint you, but I am not entirely devoted to scribbling. I have one rather special talent. I'm pretty much in favor with the . . . powers that be, and as long as I have my—er—spirit connections, as you might call them, Mark Thursten is going to make me welcome whenever I care to visit Beach House. . . . You see, a great deal about me has come to Mark's ears since you talked with me last."

That really shook me. "What? Mark despises that sort of thing. Ouija boards and séances, all that claptrap."

His devilish dark eyebrows arched in polite contradiction. "Ask him," he advised me. "Go ahead. Ask Mark if he doesn't want to contact his wife from—wherever she may be. And I am his key to that whole . . . shall we call it that other world?"

I didn't even stop to dignify that with a denial. It was too sick, too horrible. Surely a mature, level-headed man like Mark Thursten didn't dabble in spiritualism! The idea offended me—and at the same time frightened me. Because, like a great many other people, I was convinced I didn't believe in ghosts—but I didn't want to put my disbelief to the test. I pounded up the steps just as Mark himself pushed the door open wide for me.

"Good, Livia. You've just time to wash up before dinner."

There was a slight stir behind me on the darkened beach. I heard Mark's quick, catching breath.

"Who is it? Who are you out there?"

"It's that man Bates," I explained.

To my surprise, Mark said with definite interest, "Oh? Good. Bates, my sister-in-law tells me you've had some rather astonishing results in psychic communication, and you might oblige us one night soon."

In the brisk, salty dark behind me, I heard Bates' ironic, amused little chuckle. "Anytime you say, Thursten."

I groaned privately, pleading with Mark in silence: "Don't do it. Don't put yourself in his hands."

But Mark went calmly on, as if he found nothing strange about Bates and his talent, "Where can we contact you?"

"I'll be around. I'm easy to find."

That was ambiguous, to say the least! But I had enough sense to keep quiet. Mark ushered me into the house and casually locked the lanai door. I wondered if he remained as conscious as I of the strange young man who stood outside, watching us with those expressive if deadly eyes. How far into the night would he stay there, in the safe, shrouded dark, watching us?

When I came back out into the hall after washing up and making myself presentable, I noticed that an electric light was on in the suite across from my room, and with a kind of dread that I tried to shake off I wondered which of the family was using Sybil Thursten's immaculate white chamber tonight.

Carol and Mark were already at the dining room table when I came in, and I suspected, noting the schoolgirlish stares she kept stealing at Mark, that I must look equally silly in my own infatuation.

I was seated between Mrs. Jeffrey's chair at the foot of the table and Bobbie's empty place at Mark's right. Bobbie and Mrs. Jeffrey came in from the back of the house, whispering together in a very impolite way. I had no doubt the girl was telling her all that had happened during our meeting with Bates. Bobbie took the chair her father held out for her and scrambled into place, showing a length of bronzed limb below her blue shorts.

When no one said anything, I broke the silence, unable to keep still any longer. "I do wonder about that writer. He's always hanging around. Bobbie and I met him outside a while ago, behaving rather oddly, I thought. Just before you saw him, Mark."

Mark started to speak. I was eager to know what he would say, but Carol cut in with her soft, whispery, hyperfeminine voice that annoyed me no end, "But that's ingratitude, Miss Carter. He's hanging around here partly because of you. I asked him earlier this afternoon if he was here about a séance. He's very good, you know." Her soft pale lips parted in a melancholy smile. "He said he was hanging around partly because Mark might want to see him and"—she shrugged as Mark glanced at her—"well, *he* said it. I didn't! He said he was also waiting for your ... girl friend. He asked me if I didn't think Livia was enchanting. He said he was waiting for Livia to come out and meet him again when she got free of—'the old man.'"

There was a dreadful silence. Nobody looked at Mark, least of all me.

Eight

"I don't even know this man's full name," I said finally. "And I doubt if he said any such thing. He is much more interested in the Jeffreys, would be my guess."

Mark stared down the table at Carol; then his gaze flickered over me. Was it my imagination, or did he hesitate just a fraction of time, as if doubtful of my loyalty, my devotion to him?

Carol and Bobbie seemed tongue-tied at my veiled accusation, but Mrs. Jeffrey managed to muster up an answer. "Really, young woman!" she said in an annoyed voice. "I've already explained to my son-in-law the service this man can do us. He has a rare ability to raise spirit contacts."

Mark drank some water, casually set the glass down, and agreed, with what I felt was an implied rebuke at me, "Ada may well be right; so let's forget Bates for the moment. He may have a real talent. We don't know yet."

I knew, from general gossip in Mark Thursten's office, that Beach House had been the scene of séances in the past. We had supposed that Mrs. Thursten, the volatile Sybil, was responsible for these Halloween capers. Now I was shaken again by the possibility that Mark himself had been a serious party to his wife's psychic experiments.

The dinner with its delicately prepared Japanese dishes, exquisitely served, should have cheered me up. I like good food as well as anyone, and Mrs. Tomei had worked hard, but all the while I ate, I kept thinking of these open and covert enemies of mine at the table. Somehow, to judge by Mark's coolness toward me at dinner, they had already infected him against me. Carol's nasty remark about the "old man," which I had thought might react against her, seemed to have made Mark think less of me. It was unfair!

He called me into the study after dinner and explained that a great deal of work had piled up during what he called euphemistically his "absence." By working with his assistants and a man brought in from the Coast, I had managed to help clear away the routine material while he was away, but he was quite right. We did have a lot of work stacked up that night, and since neither of us appeared to feel sociable, we got through it rapidly. I took much of his dictation directly on the typewriter, so this eliminated one step. Though I knew we were behaving with great efficiency, I felt almost sick over his coolness toward me.

But even in a bad or preoccupied mood, Mark was thoughtful of his employees. He interrupted himself several times to ask if I cared for a coffee break, or if I wanted to take a stretch. My own spirits remained pretty low; I refused any breaks and we finished shortly before eleven. He signed the letters, which would be picked up in the morning for mailing by someone from town, and his severe features softened as he handed them to me.

"What would I do without you, Livia?" he asked with the warmth for which I'd been yearning.

Because I was nervous, embarrassed, and hopeful, all at the same time, I treated his remark more lightly than I felt. "It's really nothing. Almost anyone can do it with their eyes closed."

He reached for my hand, squeezed it between his own strong fingers, and did my heart a lot of good by denying what I'd said. "I don't believe that for a minute." He laughed and let my hand go gently. "You've even shared my ostracism. Don't think I'm not aware of the suspicions against you. They may have been absurd, but they were no less painful."

It bothered me a little that he should find absurd the idea of our being possible lovers. As long as I had been suspected in some quarters and had suffered from that, I wished Mark would at least find it plausible that people should imagine him in love with me. A minute later, I hoped I had one explanation, at least, for his feeling. Or lack of it!

"As if a child barely out of her teens would be involved with a widower twice her age!"

"You're not twice my age," I contradicted angrily. "That's ridiculous!"

He laughed. "How sensitive the young are about their youth!" He simply could not grasp what really bothered me. However, he got up then and put his arm around me and we walked out of the study together in a delightfully companionable way.

"Shall we invade Mrs. Tomei's kitchen and make ourselves a snack?" he suggested. "I think we've earned it."

No delights are a hundred percent satisfactory in this imperfect world, so I made do with what I had—Mark's fatherly friendship and consideration for me. But I thought wryly, "Even that sinister young Bates acts as if he sees that I am a woman, which is more than you do."

The house seemed filled with odd sounds, either because a night wind had blown up, or because the old place was still settling. There were all sorts of creaking noises, and several times I looked around or jumped nervously before we reached the kitchen. A tray containing a coffee cup, a bottle, and a sugar bowl had been left on the counter; one of the glass percolators was perking, and the big room smelled deliciously of fresh coffee.

"Makes it almost worth working late," Mark said, getting down a second cup and pouring coffee for us both. The domesticity of the scene, repeated for the second night in a row, was even more gratifying to me than the coffee itself. While I sipped, I watched him over the rim of my cup. He seemed far away; something about this late-evening coffee klatch must have brought back a memory. With a sick and wholly unfair jealousy, I guessed he was remembering when he had shared such moments with Sybil. His eyes had a vague, sad, distant look, as if he hardly saw me.

I set my cup down softly because I felt like an intruder. It seemed to me that my childish mood tainted everything. Even the coffee seemed bitter.

Mark saw my gesture and remarked in a low voice, "She was really something of a night creature, you know. She loved this sort of thing. She could stay up—dance all night. Or walk. Sometimes it used to disturb me. I'd leave my study, expect to find her upstairs preparing for bed. All the lamps on in that beautiful white shrine of hers. . . . And all the time she'd been out striding up and down the beach ... her lovely hair blowing in the sea breeze. . . . Funny," he mused, finishing his coffee mechanically. "Funny that she should have died like that—"

Startled, I asked, "What do you mean?"

He shrugged. "To die like that. A clumsy fall from those steps. It must have been like that. And yet she was strong, and she walked those steps, in the dark, many times. It's all so incredible."

Until this minute I had continued to believe, in spite of many moments of doubt, that Sybil Thursten's death must have been accidental, since the only murder suspect had been with me at the time of her death. But now those doubts were growing into conviction. Suppose someone else had a motive for her death. Why not? She was a beautiful woman with a handsome husband. Two motives there: someone jealous of her—someone who cared for him as I did; or a man who loved her and had been jilted.

Mark reacted to my expression and teased me lightly. "You look as if you had discovered the world's best-kept secret."

"No. I was just thinking—isn't it possible Mrs. Thursten really was murdered? That blow on her forehead?" When Mark frowned, I rushed on. "Some man who had been seeing her on those walks? Or—"

His harsh reply shook me: "I don't believe

it! You're merely thinking this because of Bobbie's testimony. But someone convinced her of that lie. You know it as well as I do. She didn't even tell the story until three days after Sybil was dead."

"Of course," I put in eagerly. "Suppose *that someone* was guilty! Don't you see? It would explain all those hateful actions. Everything!"

He appeared to consider this, but I could see he wasn't buying it. Nor did he want me to pursue that line, because—as I belatedly saw—by suspecting Sybil's family I somehow soiled the dead woman.

"No, Livia. It's too fantastic. I knew Sybil and her family when Carol was no older than young Bobbie. All the Jeffreys have always been deeply devoted to each other. There could never be a motive strong enough for either Ada or Carol to raise a finger against my wife."

Seeing that his mood was somber again, I tried once more. "Maybe it was somebody we don't know. Some—beachcomber?" But I was losing my impetus and my enthusiasm for detective work. Either the coffee had been too strong, or Mark's mood was contagious.

He asked in mild surprise, "Come now, Livy, when have you seen a sinister beachcomber on Oahu? These aren't the South Seas, you know. . . . Shall we adjourn and get some sleep? I have several Australian shipping charts I want

117

to get to tomorrow, and I can't make head or tail of them without your help."

He turned out the kitchen lights and made a wide, friendly gesture, inviting me to go before him. I started along the hall but, unexpectedly, he put his arm—warm and welcome—around my shoulders. He stopped me briefly, looking down into my face.

"You look a trifle done in. I shouldn't have kept you up so late. Don't get up in the morning until you're ready. I don't want you wearing yourself to a shadow on my account."

I was feeling just as done in as I looked, my stomach nervous and shaky and even my head beginning to ache, but when I contradicted him: "No, no. I loved it!" he kissed me in the gentlest way, and I felt this alone was worth a thousand pains.

We saw no one on the lower floor, but as we started up the front stairs I heard a sharp crackling sound, which seemed to come from the darkened living room. I paused abruptly and Mark did too, on the landing. He looked back. I suspected my nervousness was catching.

"The fire," he said after listening a second or two. "It must be dying out. I hope Bobbie had fun with it. I got the wood from out back."

There was silence then, and we went on to our rooms. I, for one, was glad enough to do so now. I was feeling decidedly rocky. I told myself I needed a restful night's sleep, but Mark's mention of his daughter made me think of something he should watch at times like this.

At the door of my bedroom I said suddenly, "I think Bobbie needs her father now, even more than your company needs you. After all, this was the whole purpose of having the Jeffreys here at Beach House, because Bobbie wouldn't come without them. And now—to leave her alone in the evenings—" I tried to soften this with a smile, although I was feeling so debilitated that even smiling was difficult. "Next time, maybe you should sit with Bobbie while she enjoys her fire."

"I believe you're right. Good night, my dear." He momentarily erased all my pains by another light kiss on my overwarm cheek. "Get a good rest."

I went into my room leaning back against the now closed door to relive that moment. But I was feeling so muddled I couldn't seem to think clearly. I decided that Mark was right. I needed rest.

I showered, hoping the needle spray would at least clear up my fuzzy brain. It didn't help. When I crawled into bed I was hurting all over, and began to wonder if I was coming down with some rare tropical disease. In a sort of daze, I chewed an antacid tablet and swallowed two aspirins.

Thus fortified, I managed to doze off briefly, but I had dreams, full of shadowy rooms, psychic manifestations, and great personal discomfort. All of this was presided over by a pallid face floating in ectoplasm, pierced by two hypnotic dark eyes that both attracted and frightened me.

Sometime during this period of discomfort that gradually verged on terror, I became aware of a door opening and closing somewhere out in the hall. With an unpleasant jarring note that further acted on my nerves, the opening and closing door began to be associated for me with the suite across the hall, the bedroom of the dead woman.

My sleep had been interrupted by interludes of headache, stomachache, and extraordinary thirst: now I seemed to be in a kind of trance or half-awakened state. Even though I was aware that I was suffering, aware too that Beach House itself seemed curiously alive around me, I still couldn't seem to shake myself into action.

I heard faint sounds in the darkness of my unfamiliar room, a coarse straining for breath, an occasional groan. At the same time I had a dream that seemed half reality, a dream of my body being consumed by flame, of the hideous pricking of little fires. The dream at last awoke me to my predicament. I was suffering from what felt like a fiery rash, though when I snapped on the light my skin looked its usual sunburned tan, with the single addition of gooseflesh.

"I've been poisoned!" I thought. And instead of calming down and thinking about what to do first, I began to shake with a palsy that affected even my teeth. I sat up in the strange bed and hugged my trembling body, trying at the same time to throw off the drugging effects of sleep. Dizzily, I looked around the room. There was no telephone extension. I vaguely remembered seeing one somewhere in the hall. It seemed a very long distance to go, almost an impossible distance. I cleared my throat, and the hoarse, retching noise grated on my ragged nerves. It sounded so unlike me that I managed to swivel my head around to stare fearfully into the unknown corners of the room. I couldn't identify half the objects I saw; they all looked vague and menacing. But it hardly mattered. I was too sick to care.

I stumbled out of bed. My knees buckled, but I managed to get to the door. My fingers were horribly stiff and dry, but they finally turned the old-fashioned glass knob, and I lurched into the hall, whispering hoarsely, "Help me! Please . . . help me!"

I had terrible grinding pains in my stomach and the joints of my body. It was too dark to see anything in the hall, but there was a rim of light under the door of Sybil's bedroom, and I staggered across the hall toward it.

121

I fell against the door, my ears closed to all sounds but the slow beat of my own pulse. The door was ajar, and I fell forward into the room. The rich, cloying scent of her perfume was thick in the air. As I lay huddled on the floor, with my hot, dry face pressed against the white nap of her rug, I imagined I heard her move toward me, felt her kneel over me. . . . Her spirit was all-pervasive. . . .

"She can't be—" I heard myself whisper through cracked and dry lips. "She can't be here. She is dead and buried. Dead. . . ."

Nine

They told me later I wasn't found until shortly before one A.M., when Mark went into his dead wife's bedroom—he said he'd heard some sort of noise in there—and found me writhing and groaning in a heap on the floor. He hadn't heard me from the hall. No one else was in the room, and there were no signs that anyone had ever been in there with me. I figured later that I had imagined Sybil Thursten's presence, although Mark didn't brush the idea aside as everyone else did, and he pursued the subject when I was recovering. He even mentioned parapsychology and hinted that our friend Bates might find me mediumistic.

By mid-afternoon of that day I could sit up in bed. I wasn't eating solid food yet, but I was well enough to be very curious about what had caused my illness. Neither the maids nor nice, sympathetic Mrs. Tomei would tell me, but Mrs. Tomei seemed to feel it was all her fault, an idea that baffled me. The minute I remembered my suspicion that I had been poisoned, I was sure one of the Jeffreys had done it. How disappointed they must be that I had survived! This remark was on the tip of my tongue when Mark came in that afternoon to see how I was, and to keep me from turning away the maid who brought me revolting concoctions prescribed by a Dr. Wong.

"Hello, Livia. How is our sick girl?" Mark looked so worried that I was quite touched. When he took up my hand and started to massage it, I made no objection. I enjoyed it, in fact.

"I'm okay," I said languidly, giving some thought to various painful spots. "Will you please tell me what happened last night?"

"I can't tell you how sorry I am. But it seems you swallowed some arsenic. Probably by mistake."

"Mistake!" I sat up indignantly, pulling my hand away. "There was no mistake about it. I was poisoned, I tell you! Why would I take arsenic—ugh—of my own accord?"

"Now . . . now. Mrs. Tomei is very upset. But it was an unfortunate accident, she says." Mark was treating me exactly as I had seen him treat Bobbie, and I resented it.

"How could I take arsenic by *mistake*?"

"Probably by mistaking it for sugar. And anyway"—he was both embarrassed and deeply concerned for me—"I may have poisoned you myself. The rodent poison Mrs. Tomei had ordered was not put away in its proper place. One of the girls opened it and left it on the kitchen shelf. Somehow, you got it in the coffee last night, probably."

That sounded possible, and it did seem an awfully roundabout way for anyone to poison me deliberately. As an idea came to me, I opened my eyes wider, although, strangely enough, even my eye muscles hurt.

"You know, Mark, you might have drunk that coffee and that arsenic yourself. There was one cup sitting there. Remember? You didn't look into it. You just poured. It might have been yours if I hadn't happened to come in with you."

I was surprised when he didn't deny this or even look startled. He nodded slowly.

"I wish it had been my cup. You're a pretty slight little girl to be taking a dose of arsenic. If the mistake had to be made, I should have taken it."

"Thank you. I'm glad you didn't." I hesitated, thinking it over. "Do we know for sure that that's how I got the arsenic?"

He looked around the room thoughtfully. "Unless you ate or drank something elsewhere." I shook my head. "Then Dr. Wong believes it was a small dose. Certainly not enough to be fatal."

"Thanks a lot!"

"I know." He leaned over me and kissed my forehead. "Don't worry, Livy. No more mistakes. Just in case, we'll be extra careful about everything you eat or drink. Now, get some sleep. We're all expecting you to be downstairs for a little while tonight. Incidentally, they've all been very concerned about you."

"I can imagine!" I thought, but didn't say so to Mark. I wondered if he really was as unsuspecting as he seemed. I rather thought he was trying to lull me, so that I wouldn't worry about other possible attempts on my life. Or had it been an attempt on *my* life? I thought my point about the possibility of Mark's being the intended victim had been glossed over too easily.

"They've all asked if they can see you for a minute or two. What do you say, Livia?"

I felt a little like a half-eaten Christian being asked to entertain more lions, but I nodded agreement. To tell the truth, I was angry enough and curious enough to want to see the Jeffreys. With the confidence of youth, and a repertoire of late-late murder movies to draw on, I thought I might guess, from the guilty person's attitude, which of them had been responsible for substituting rat poison for sugar. And if I couldn't pick the guilty person, then remembering those terrible hours last night, I made up my mind I'd leave Beach House if I had to crawl away!

I half expected Bobbie to come in first and chatter away, whether to conceal the truth or not, I couldn't foresee. But instead, Carol Jeffrey came in first, and alone. She seemed much more upset than I had expected her to be. After all, we had been virtual rivals since Mark chose me for his secretary instead of her. There was no reason for her to care whether I lived or died. If she still believed I had lied in giving Mark an alibi for her sister's death, then she ought to be happy over my close call.

Her usually clean, shiny hair was dishevelled; her scrubbed face now had a mottled, sick look. She even stammered a little.

"I—I . . . Mark says you got hold of some rat poison. That—that's rough."

I watched her closely, wondering whether she was frightened because of her own guilt or because she really didn't know what had happened. It was hard to tell. At her remark I shrugged. The movement was still painful. My joints felt stiff. The discomfort made me resent more than ever what had happened to me.

"I wonder who it was intended for," I said coolly. "Besides rats, I mean." Carol flushed a little, and chewed her lower lip. I thought she was about to contradict me, and I headed her off bitterly. "Not that there are rats around

here. They always insist there aren't any danger-
ous creatures like that in Hawaii."

"Snakes," Carol put in lamely. "It's poi-
sonous snakes we're short of. . . . Look here,
Livia, I'm sorry. I really am." She took a deep
breath, wet her lips. They looked nearly as dry
as my own. "But it was an accident. Mrs. Tomei says—"

"I know. It happens all the time. People always leave roach powder and ant and rat poison
on kitchen shelves beside the food."

"Well, they do!" she said defensively. "Mrs.
Tomei says she ordered it. Somehow the powder got mixed up with the sugar, or . . . something or other."

I said nothing because I was too busy
watching her. She wasn't at all like the suspects
in the late-late show. She looked as if she were
suffering, as if she believed all that about acci-
dents and mixing the poison package with the
newly arrived food staples by mistake. But
when I didn't agree with her, she finally stammered to a stop and looked anxiously at the
door. Probably she had set herself to be polite
for ten minutes before leaving the floor to her
mother or Bobbie.

I decided to give her at least one shock before she left. I said in a pleasanter voice, "You
may be right. It wasn't intended that I get that
arsenic compound, or whatever it was. . . ."

"No. Of course not." She was noticeably encouraged. "That's what I said. Mother told Mrs. Tomei that."

"Because," I went on firmly, "that coffee cup was intended for Mark."

She cried out. "What? That's a horrible thing to say! You must be crazy. I can understand someone trying to get it straight about a questionable death that's already occurred. But to do a thing like that to Mark, when he's been so good to us all, in spite of everything!" Carol seemed in such a panic that I almost felt guilty at having considered the idea. At the same time, it angered me to think that an attempt to poison Mark would be so much more shocking to her than my own possible murder. I turned my head on the pillow and stared at the wall until she took the hint and got up to leave. She surprised me by hesitating briefly in the doorway.

"Anyway—I'm sorry. Mother is sorry too. That's—that's about all. Except, everyone's being awfully careful about the food now, especially yours. I thought you'd like to know."

I did like to know. The trouble was, I couldn't trust anyone to mean it. I wanted to believe, but couldn't quite, that last night's poisoning was just the result of a mixup in packages. The fact that Carol might be innocent of the whole thing was gratifying. But it hadn't kept the thing from happening, and the question remained, for me, of whether the ar-

129

senic had been possibly meant for me or for Mark. Or maybe for us both.

Even though it probably wasn't Carol's fault, her visit jarred me more than I'd expected it would. I found that it was hard to look a distraught person in the eye and argue with myself about whether she was a killer or not. After Carol had gone, I tried to stop shaking, but it wasn't long before I heard the usual creaks and cracks out in the hall, which told me that more than one person was hanging around my door.

"Come in!" I called angrily, wanting to get any more unpleasant interviews out of the way quickly.

"Let me! Let me!" Bobbie Thursten cried in her shrill young voice a minute after she came in carrying a covered tray. One of the part-time maids hired by Mrs. Tomei stuck her pert dark head in the doorway behind Bobbie.

"Is it all right, Miss Carter? Miss Bobbie wants to feed you."

I was still too stupefied at Bobbie's nerve to say anything. I just stared while Bobbie bounced over to my bed and set the tray down on my knees. She looked eager and hopeful as she announced, "I'm going to sample every single thing you eat. I'm your official taster! Now! What do you say to that?"

I grinned weakly, but she meant it. Before I could stop her, she picked up a tall glass filled with a milky medicinal substance and sipped it, wrinkling her nose.

"Honest, Livy, we're innocent! I swear it! The scuttlebutt is that you think we all tried to poison you. What do we have to do to convince you?"

"Yes, Miss Carter," came Mrs. Jeffrey's cold, clipped voice from the open doorway. "What must we do to convince you?"

Bobbie glanced quickly over her shoulder and looked at her grandmother. For a brief instant I thought the girl seemed troubled, but she recovered her almost desperate gaiety at once.

"Anyway, let's get on to the juice." She sampled that too, but I was more interested in watching Mrs. Jeffrey's movements. She came into the room rather uncertainly, I thought, though her face was as fixed and stern as ever.

"But she can't be the one!" I thought. "She's so obvious. If she'd really done it she'd be playing it cool, pretending to be concerned."

And she certainly wasn't doing that. Every time I looked at her I saw the icy contempt, the unbending implacability of a fanatic. She was impossible either to like or to dismiss. Even when my back was turned, I felt her dislike stabbing me between the shoulder blades.

"You've proved your point," I told Bobbie, and began to drink the nauseating white stomach calmer.

Bobbie looked hopefully at her grandmother. I was sure she was asking the woman to break down and say something conciliatory, but instead, Mrs. Jeffrey said brusquely, "Leave us together, Barbara. I want to have a little chat with Miss Carter."

The idea of finding myself alone with the old basilisk in my present weakened condition put me in a panic. "No! Wait!" I tried to catch Bobbie by a shirt-sleeve, but she was moving too quickly. She was too used to obeying her grandmother.

"Run along, Barbara," Mrs. Jeffrey said firmly.

"Okay." And she went out into the hall. I was relieved when I saw that she intended to wait beside the door, leaning negligently on one elbow against the wall.

Mrs. Jeffrey carefully closed the door. It was so slow and deliberate a gesture that I wondered if it was intended as a snub to her granddaughter. Watching her, I managed a distinctly hollow laugh.

"You're being very secretive, but I warn you, I have a very loud scream."

She turned to me at last, with a contemptuous twist of her thin lips. "Don't trouble yourself. I shan't be long." Nevertheless, when she moved purposefully around the foot of my bed toward me, I had a cowardly impulse to curl up and draw away from her.

"I want to know something, young woman. And I don't mean to be put off."

I tried to interrupt her to say that I had a few things to ask on my own behalf, but my tongue felt thick and my mouth was so dry I couldn't get out a word.

"What were you doing in my daughter's room last night?"

I croaked out that the light had been on, and she looked hard at me, as if she could read my mind. Perhaps she could.

"Did you see anyone in that room? Come, speak up! What did you see there?"

I remembered those awful moments on the floor in Sybil Thursten's bedroom, when I had imagined the dead woman was bending over me. But I had been in such pain I couldn't recall now what was nightmare and what was real. I drank a few sips of water, trying to calm myself. Mrs. Jeffrey watched me with such concentration that I stopped abruptly and stared at the glass. In sudden horror I wondered if even the water could be poisoned.

Sheer anger at her nerve made me recover more rapidly then than I might have. I tried again and got my voice working.

"I know someone bent over me. Someone was there. I don't know who it was. It could have been anyone."

"Even a man?"

"I suppose. The room was so full of Mrs.

Thursten's perfume that anyone coming in might be mistaken for her if I didn't see—" A man? What did she mean? There was no man in the house except Mark.

She turned away from me, flexing her fingers nervously. She seemed less certain of herself now, and I, by contrast, felt more able to handle her. "Mrs. Jeffrey, what is it you want from me? What did you think I saw last night?"

She swung around, still moving her thin hard fingers as if she could not control them. But her eyes were not so fierce. They looked watery, even anxious. "It has been brought to my attention that you may have psychic vibrations, Miss Carter. Without knowing it, you may possess some gift for contact with the other side."

"Me? Contact with what other side?" I hoped I had misunderstood her.

"The dead. In short ... my daughter Sybil. You may have been contacted by her last night during your illness and not have realized it."

I had an awful feeling that she meant this, and I fumbled for a way out. But she interrupted my mumbled protests to say calmly, "You will help us. Because you must."

She opened the door while I was still demanding to know why and wondering how I could get out of this.

"Because, young lady, you claim you did not lie when you took the witness stand. If that is true, you should have no reason to fear my daughter. If it is a lie—" She shrugged, leaving no doubt as to what I might expect from the world beyond.

"All set, Gram?" Bobbie asked as Mrs. Jeffrey joined her in the hall. I didn't hear the reply. My door was closed abruptly.

Trembling violently, I laid the tray on the floor and sat up in bed, trying to restore some kind of calm, but I was scared to death. No matter how much Mrs. Jeffrey insisted that if I had told the truth I would have nothing to fear, I wanted no part of any meeting with the dead Sybil. And I *had* thought that I'd seen her.

A short while later, when the maid came to take away the tray, she found me dizzily trying to run a bath, and stopped her other work long enough to finish the job for me. Her dark eyes sparkled.

"Is it true, miss, there's going to be a séance here one night soon?"

I said I didn't know and I thought, "Not if I can help it," but I was beginning to discover that my dragging heels wouldn't even slow the momentum. The Jeffreys were determined to hold a séance, and apparently they had convinced Mark that it was worth a try. If it weren't for my anxiety to please him, I would have packed up and left that minute, before any more dead people were called in from the "other side."

No one was in the hall when I walked shakily out of my room. I had a terrific urge to go outside and lie on the warm beach in the sun. I still had moments of shivering; my skin felt unnaturally dry, and my joints gave me the impression they needed oiling. I decided that if I did stay here another night, I would go swimming tomorrow. It was too late to drive back to Honolulu today, even if I felt like it.

When I walked down the beach steps, I saw Mark up on the road by the half-built garage, talking to a stout dark man. At the same time Joe Nakazawa, who had taken a break to smoke a cigarette, waved to me and started to stride down the sandy slope toward me. I walked halfway to meet him. I was probably happier to see him than he was to see me. Not only was he the liveliest person in the neighborhood, but the only one who appeared totally unconnected with the strange doings at Beach House.

However, the Beach House excitement, which I could do without, was obviously Joe's big interest.

"Hi! I hear you had a real winger last night," he greeted me enthusiastically. "Who do you suppose it was meant for?"

I correctly assumed he was talking about the rodent killer that had gotten into my coffee, and, in a perverse mood, I denied any foul play.

But Joe was skeptical. "Yeah, maybe. Just the same, how come Mr. Thursten's up there giving everyone's life history to a detective?"

"Detective!" I stared at the distant figures with new apprehension. The presence of the law suddenly crystallized my fear. Until this minute, beneath all my melodramatic concern, I had secretly hoped that it really had been a kitchen accident, some clumsy mixing up of outdoor and indoor supplies. But the presence of a real live detective, and the memory of Mark's very concerned look, did away with that hope completely.

"Tell me," I said suddenly, lowering my voice in a conspiratorial manner that wasn't all a put-on, "Joe, if you're sure that was a real attempt to poison someone, who do *you* think is responsible?"

"*Who* is the guilty party?" he declaimed, grinning. But he probably read the anxiety in my eyes, because he looked over his shoulder, then took me by the arm and led me further away from the house. "There's a joker been hanging around here a lot lately. Come from the vets' hospital. If you ask me, that guy's a psycho. Stands to reason."

I inhaled with a big gasp. "You mean Bates? I think so too. Or I did. But that business last night came from inside the house. I don't see how Bates could have switched the kitchen packages around."

"Don't tell me! Listen! I was over the Makai Point last night because my uncle had a big notion to go spearfishing. Never caught anything but a sore toe from the coral. Anyway, about ten o'clock last night, who should be leaving down those lanai steps but Pretty Boy Bates! Uncle Ito figures the guy'd been visiting somebody at Beach House. I thought that *haole* looked sneaky. But Uncle Ito's toe was giving him so much trouble we didn't challenge the guy."

Another complication. I had been wondering since my meeting with Bates late yesterday if I could trust him. It would have been nice to eliminate at least one suspect.

I heard Joe's name called and we both looked around. Then Mark saw me and waved. He said something to the detective, and they started down toward us. I wanted to run away. I didn't feel sure enough of anyone yet to answer questions.

"It's all right, Livia. Padilla won't bite," Mark said when they reached us. He held out his hand and I took it gratefully. "Miss Carter, Conrad Padilla. He is helping us find out just how you got that dose of rat poison. I think we should know, don't you, dear?"

"It—wasn't a mistake?" I asked, almost hoping still that they would contradict me.

Mark glanced at Joe Nakazawa, who gave a light, almost flippant salute and went off to gather up his tools. I wondered if he could hear our conversation.

"I'm afraid we can't be sure," Mark said, looking down thoughtfully at our hands, still clasped together. "There seems to be some doubt about who was intended to be poisoned, but not about the intention itself."

The heavy-faced detective, Mr. Padilla, shook his head. I found the three of us walking toward the kitchen entry door and thought suddenly of Bates and what Joe Nakazawa had said about him, that he had been in a veterans' hospital, that he was mentally unstable: "psycho," Joe had called him. Had he sneaked into the kitchen last night while Mark and I were working in the study? But if he had, his visit couldn't have been kept entirely secret. Carol or Mrs. Jeffrey or Bobbie, or more than one of them, had been in the living room, around the fire. It was hardly likely that Bates could have passed them without being seen.

Detective Padilla turned to me unexpectedly. "What is your recollection of the coffee business last night, Miss Carter? The precise details, if you can tell us."

Mrs. Tomei glanced out a kitchen window, smiled at me, and then, seeing Mr. Padilla, she looked apprehensively from him to the interior of the kitchen. She must have recognized Padilla, because she disappeared from the window and came rushing to the entry door.

"An accident, sir! I swear. An accident so stupid! We would not hurt the young lady or Mister Mark. Mister Mark has always been our friend. Since early days."

Mark and I both tried to console her together, but Mr. Padilla paid no attention. He cut directly into my assurances. "Will you be so good as to act out the business of the coffee? And the sugar? Especially the sugar? It may be that you were not the target, as we've surmised, Miss Carter. We want to be sure."

I stepped into the entry ahead of him, past the big refrigerator, and started to point out where we had entered from the hall and where I had stood as Mark reached for the second cup. I had barely got started when I found myself speechless.

Sitting on a stool beside the cupboards, and looking as friendly as you please, was Bates, his dark eyes scanning me from head to foot.

"Glad to see you up and around, Livy. This is what comes of too much coffee nerves. You should stick to milk."

Startled, Mark glanced at me and then at Bates again. He had called me Livy in a ridiculous and impudent way. At any other time I would have hoped Mark was jealous. Now, after Joe's story, I was too unnerved at the way Bates seemed to be so much at home in the room where I had been poisoned.

Ten

Mr. Padilla was not impressed either by Bates' impudence or his charms. He said brusquely, "Your name?"

"Dion Bates, sir." He looked so humble, and spoke so politely, that I would almost have believed he was as innocent as he sounded, but when he glanced briefly at me, the old mischievous light was there; so attractive, so hypnotic, that I realized I had almost fallen into his usual trap. He got up, made a little waving motion with one hand. "Please have my seat. I was just trying to wheedle a snack from my friend Mrs. Tomei."

Little Mrs. Tomei smiled shyly at him. It was clear that she was influenced, as I was, by the man's personal attractions. He did not have Mark's maturity and reserve, but I found myself responding to his good looks and impudent charm, and I knew I had identified with a younger man for the first time. Until this minute I hadn't believed Mark was right when he spoke of the age gap between us, but now I thought I understood him. I was still young enough to find myself affected by the appeal of surface attractions. Perhaps I really wasn't mature enough for Mark.

Mark explained calmly to Mr. Padilla, "Mr. Bates is a friend of my sister-in-law, Carol Jeffrey. He is leaving now."

Looking a trifle startled, Bates agreed in haste and began to back out of the kitchen, making mumbled excuses, which I suspected were his private joke. Then he looked my way at the last minute and I saw that his expression was far more intense than I had supposed. And I remembered that ugly word Joe had used so casually: "psycho." I was surprised at my own disappointment, maybe because the mysterious Dion Bates had appeared to be softening in his attitude toward me, and it is only human for a girl to hope an extraordinarily handsome man will find her attractive. I certainly was ambivalent about him.

To get my mind off the departed Bates, I began to talk rapidly, demonstrating as I did so.

"We came in from the hall. Here. We were alone." To Padilla's question I added, "We didn't see or hear anyone, did we, Mark?"

He had been studying the hall doorway thoughtfully and when I repeated my assertion he agreed, but I wondered whether he had been recalling some sound, some possible listener or watcher who might have been near.

"Anyway, there was one cup laid out by Mrs. Tomei. You see, she thought Mark would be coming in alone for coffee after he finished his work."

We all looked at the cook, who was busy scrubbing the walls of the big storage freezer in the narrow kitchen entry. She inclined her head, smiling agreeably. She might not even have heard us.

"Yes, yes. I have her story." Detective Padilla dismissed her impatiently and turned again to me.

I repeated as well as I could remember every move we had made last night, and my account seemed to check with Mark's recollections. I felt sure, from the way the detective looked at me and then at Mark, as if mentally double-checking, that I had been wise not to leave out a single detail. To me it now added up to a clear case of an attempt to poison Mark, which had backfired because he'd behaved like a gentleman and given me the first cup he touched.

Detective Padilla then hinted that since Mark had given me the cup, Mark, in a sense, could be guilty. Mark was startled, but had to agree that he had actually given me the poisoned coffee. No one seemed likely to be eavesdropping on this conversation, but if someone had been, I thought, the Jeffreys or Dion Bates would have been highly amused at Padilla's briefly expounded theory. Nothing would make them happier than for suspicions to develop between Mark and me.

I was relieved when Detective Padilla left. I wondered what he really thought, and if he was actually trying to make me suspicious of Mark.

After Padilla had driven off, Mark asked me with a frown: "What the devil do you suppose Bates was doing in the kitchen? He seems to be getting awfully familiar with the household."

I said I supposed Mrs. Tomei liked him. "And that's odd, because she told me yesterday that he was a death figure, or something like it. But then," I added, thinking out loud, "there's no getting around it. He's got a way of charming people."

"So I notice," Mark agreed with a wry little smile. He inspected my face carefully. "Are you feeling better? Your color is coming back."

I said I thought I was all right, that I was going to take it easy for an hour, and Mark, looking relieved, chucked me under the chin, exactly as if I were his thirteen-year-old daughter.

"Run along now. I'm going to dictate a few letters into that infernal machine. I'll send the tapes to the office to be transcribed; your orders are to get well and forget work."

He was being terribly sweet, but he constantly seemed to view me as if I were barely into puberty. Maybe I should dress differently. That was one thing to be said for Bates, I reflected again. He, at least, looked at me as if he found me over the age of consent. I left the kitchen hurriedly. It had unpleasant associations for me, in more than one way.

One of the pretty part-time girls, who turned out to be Mrs. Tomei's daughter, was vacuuming the shadowed living room as I went past. She gave a little scream at sight of me and snapped off the cleaner with her foot. The little vacuum light, which had been crawling over the worn carpet, went off at the same time. In any other house I would have been offended to think I scared people, but in this old Victorian horror of a house I understood perfectly.

"It's only me," I said. "Don't you find this room creepy?"

"Creepy is right." She pointed the toe of her sandal to the little vacuum light. "I'm almost afraid to turn this darn thing on, for fear of what I'm likely to see running around the floor. You know what they're going to do in this room tonight?"

"I'm afraid to ask."

She peered out into the hall. I had a feeling she shared my fear of those dark corners. Her voice was distinctly lower, and I moved closer.

"They're going to hold a séance, and from

the look of this mausoleum, they've got a million places to pop out of."

"Who?" She had me whispering too.

"But the dead ones, of course."

"Oh no! I hoped they'd forget about the séance."

She was right about the concealment the room offered—the nooks and corners, the dark woodwork of the two buttresses, which formed more shadowed squares behind them, the corner fireplace and the innumerable cushioned odds and ends of furniture. Maybe I could be too sick to attend.

"When do you leave?" I asked her.

She glanced at her wristwatch. "Half an hour."

"I'd like to trade places with you."

I meant it, too. I went up to my room. Bobbie, or somebody, was running the shower between our bedrooms; so I lay down as I was, clothes and all, on my bed. I must have dozed off, because I came to myself with a terrific jolt, to find it was dusk out and that the room was gray-dark. I lay there a minute, wondering what had aroused me with that nerve-wracking jolt. Then I remembered. It had been a noise overhead, a heavy crash, as if something, or someone, had fallen on the floor of one of the attic storerooms.

I sat up, staring at the ceiling, wishing I could see through it with X-ray eyes. I was feeling better now, and the longer I listened to the extraordinary silence around me, the more curious I became. Gradually, as I remained perfectly still, I imagined I heard shuffling sounds overhead, followed by little periods of silence, exactly as if something were being done secretly, with an effort not to be overheard.

Since they were apparently pushing hard for that séance tonight, I felt at a terrific disadvantage. In spite of the fact that the rat poison had very likely been intended for Mark, I felt dismally certain that I would be a center of attention at any séance they organized. To judge by Mrs. Jeffrey's persistence, I had been elected as their medium, and while I still remembered the awful "presence" of the dead Sybil Thursten last night in her bedroom, I refused to believe that this demonstrated any gift of extrasensory perception on my part. What it did demonstrate was the impact of a dead person's surroundings, and above all, a dead person's perfume, in evoking the presence of someone from Mrs. Jeffrey's other side.

I felt considerably stronger now after my rest, and this, combined with a righteous anger at being squeezed into a situation I fiercely resented—and feared?—made me decide to beard the enemy in his, or more likely *her*, den. I got up and went out into the hall, closing my door soundlessly, and trying to avoid the noisier floorboards of the hall. I suppose, beneath my determination and anger, there must have been fear, because I kept glancing over my shoulder, squinting to look into the dark corners of the hall. I may even have been reliving that first eerie day when I came out to Beach House alone and found Mrs. Jeffrey, like a leering goddess of death, enthroned in that attic room, as if she were waiting for me.

What had she been doing up there? Events had moved so fast since then that I'd never found out. Perhaps now was the time! I went very quietly up the circling stairs to the low-roofed attic corridor. Before I reached the attic, I found I had to feel my way. The only light at this hour between dusk and night was that which normally streamed through the west windows of the house, and most of these on the attic floor were shuttered. There was, of course, the room from which I suspected Mrs. Jeffrey had watched me that first day, but its door was closed and I saw only a dim streak of the sunset's afterglow under the door. It did help to suggest where the various other doors were, however.

The room that interested me most was the one directly over the bedroom assigned to me, which had appeared to be full of sound and fury ten minutes ago. Now it was quiet enough so that I could almost imagine my slightest sound, even my heartbeat, was heard within the low-roofed room. Like a coward I waited a few minutes, half hidden, at the top of the staircase beside the room, on the theory that I might see who came out without myself being seen.

When this prudence got me nowhere, I reached over and tried the doorknob. It gave easily under my hand and I pushed the door open, trying to get a clear view of the room without moving from my place of shelter on the staircase. It was impossible, of course. The room was shrouded in gray-dark. I drew closer to the partially open door and looked in. The room was a very small one, whose slanting roof and dormer window made it seem even smaller. It had evidently once been a bedroom; it was partially furnished with odd pieces—an old-fashioned walnut chiffonier, a bird's-eye-maple vanity table, which didn't match anything else, several chairs in various states of disrepair, and an expensive but outmoded cedar chest, which had been so carelessly closed that some of the garments inside still trailed out, halfway to the floor.

No one was in the room. I closed the door silently behind me and crossed the room. I knew that psychedelic sunburst of gold, green, and blue Thai silk which had been so hastily jammed into the chest. I had seen the hostess pajamas on Sybil Thursten at her last Beach House luau. It was one of those loud, happy outfits that suited her so well. One was likely to find her gaiety contagious, and clothes like this, which would have been vulgar on anyone else, merely enhanced her bright charm. I had almost touched the sparkling material before I felt repulsion toward it, and the guilt that went with that repulsion.

Sybil Thursten had never hurt me, not that I knew of, anyway; yet I had disliked her, been envious of her. It was probably this guilt that made everything about her so terrifying to me now.

I looked around and saw other bits of Sybil Thursten's life—a half-opened bureau drawer with slim, folded cheongsams, and then pairs of shoes whose vague outlines I made out on an open shelf. There was a pair with buckles reminiscent of the twenties that Sybil had worn one afternoon to the office when she picked up Mark and they went on to a dinner at the Royal Hawaiian Hotel. All of us in the office had envied her self-assurance; at the same time we had resented the way she looked through us as if we weren't there.

The little room began to stifle me. Even here there was the faint, stale odor of Mrs. Thursten's perfume. I suddenly had to get out. I went to the door and was about to turn the doorknob when I was startled by the soft, careful closing of a door nearby. For a second or two I was sure I had made the sound myself.

But I hadn't yet touched the doorknob. I waited, my heart thumping, as I tried to guess the location of the person who shared with me these darkening attic rooms.

It seemed forever before I made up my mind that no one was in the hall, and I stepped out, looking around with such a shaky lack of courage that I despised myself. I think I could have faced any normal confrontation here, including the formidable Mrs. Jeffrey, but my experience of the last few minutes with the inanimate "life" of the dead woman everywhere around me had reduced me to this shivering state. Also, it didn't help that it was now so dark that I could hardly see the opposite end of the hall.

I decided to open each of the attic doors, and before I could change my mind I went down the hall, this time hearing my own determined footsteps. The doors of the two small rooms on one side of the hall were locked. I gave up, and seeing a very welcome narrow servants' staircase beyond, I started down. At the attic end of the stairs it was so dark I had to feel my way, but as the stairs circled downward, the stale, perfumed darkness changed to frosty gray. Somewhere below, probably around the newel-post, was a fifteen-watt light, barely adequate, but typical of the lighting in the rear quarters of such a Victorian house. The light was still exceedingly vague, but enough so that I was able to see where to put each foot.

And now there was something else, too. Something still below my reach that blocked my way, a monolith in the half-light, immovable but no less terrifying nonetheless. I stopped with one foot feeling for the step below, knowing that what I saw was impossible and yet shaking so that I couldn't even cry out.

Sybil Thursten stood there in her green and gold Siamese stole, looking up at me with eyes dead these nearly six months, yet staring . . . staring. . . .

Everything was shadowed but those eyes, mischievous and sparkling, even in death.

I scrambled back up two steps at a time until I reached the attic floor. It was now so dark that I could see nothing at all as I stumbled along the corridor toward what I devoutly hoped was the front staircase. I put both hands out like a blind woman, felt my way past three doors, and then, hearing what sounded horribly like soft, padded footsteps behind me—but what might have been my own echo—I felt my way down the front staircase.

Lights had been turned on in the second-floor hall, and two female voices were chattering so loudly I should have been reassured, but I was nearly in a state of collapse and hardly recognized either Carol or Mrs. Jeffrey until the latter said coldly, "Young woman, kindly do not race down the stairs. Even Barbara has better manners."

"But I saw—I saw—" I got no further. They were staring at me, and I knew suddenly what it would mean if I told them the truth. They would swear I was psychic, the perfect medium for their ghastly séance. "I heard something upstairs. As if someone had fallen. But I couldn't find anyone."

Carol looked puzzled, glancing up the stairs as if she didn't quite believe me, but her mother said with her usual brisk competence, "Never mind. You had better take something to calm your nerves, Miss Carter. After dinner, that young Bates is going to entertain us. You must be sure to be at your best. How are you feeling?"

"Terrible!" I said firmly, clutching my forehead; I made a pretense of dizziness, which was only half false, and reached vaguely for my door.

Carol moved quickly toward me but I motioned her away. She murmured to her mother, "Maybe we shouldn't tonight. She really looks all in."

But Mrs. Jeffrey overruled this as if it had been a deliberate affront to her. "Don't be ridiculous. Carol, get her some water. Or something. Young lady, you have caused this family a great deal of grief. Let us hope tonight you can make up to us in some part for the harm you have done."

"Mother! For heaven's sake!" I thought Carol was going to try to console me, but I was much too unnerved to have any of that wretched family touch me.

"Leave me alone," I said without looking at them, and hurried into my room. I couldn't lock the door, but there were no more sounds near my room. The women had evidently gone away. I lay down on the bed once more and stared at the ceiling until I finally stopped shaking.

What had I seen on those back stairs a little while ago? Was it some queer phantom my fears had conjured up, something absolutely unreal, a trick of light and shadow? Or was it Sybil Thursten, incredibly, standing there, very much in the flesh?

Eleven

Every five minutes or so I would feel my body jump nervously and I would glance at the door. It seemed to me that when I was not looking at the door, just out of the corner of my eye I could see the doorknob turning gently, silently. . . . But nothing happened, and after a while I reached out and snapped on the bed-side lamp. The room looked more cheerful with the warm pink glow from the old-fashioned lampshade. I glanced at my travel clock. It was cocktail time and no one had called me. Well, maybe Mark had said, "Don't bother her. Let the child rest." It would be like him to call me "child"—he did so even at the office, when I doubly didn't enjoy it.

Fingers drummed abruptly on the door panel, something that hadn't happened since a boyfriend in junior college used to announce himself like that. I supposed it must be one of the Jeffrey women, or maybe Bobbie Thursten, because I had never known Mark to give me that boyish a summons.

"Who is it?" I called, and got for answer a repetition of that irritating sound. This time I swung out of bed, surprising myself at my equilibrium, and went to the door. I pulled it open and caught my breath in surprise. There stood Dion Bates, with a big smile and knuckles raised almost in my face, ready to try his luck a third time.

For some reason I felt my face burn with what was either anger or embarrassment. I knew I looked a wreck, but why I should care what this annoying and possibly murderous fellow thought of my looks was beyond me at the moment.

"What do *you* want?" I demanded, in what I hoped was the voice of a superior and challenging adult.

He looked over my head at the room and told me in a consciously "sensible" tone, "You can hardly be cheerful all alone in this place. A borrowed room. I came up to get you."

"Why you? What have you got to say about Mr. Thursten's house?"

He held up one palm solemnly. "I've been invited to dinner. I swear it. And when I asked why the prettiest girl in the house was sulking in her room, our noble host was too cowardly to come up and pry you loose from this hole."

I tried to cut him short with an indignant

denial that there was an ounce of cowardice in Mark Thursten's body, but this got me nowhere. He only smiled at what he called my "insufferable hero worship of older men," then pushed me aside quite easily and entered my room.

"Come on, Livy. Be good. Only you can make my day. Where is your lipstick? Shall I zip you up or unzip you, as the case may be?"

It was not a bit of use to argue with him. That would only bring Mark, and I didn't want to upset him. Besides, I felt that Bates' visit to me, in spite of his impudent approach, really might be a deliberate effort to pull me out of the doldrums and get me downstairs to dinner. If so, it was rather charming of him. I found I preferred to believe he meant well. I didn't tell him so in those words, however.

"Don't be silly. Go on back downstairs. I'll be down in a minute." Just to show him his place in the scheme of things, I added, "Tell Mark that." I closed the door and hurried around making myself look a little bit more presentable.

When I went out into the hall ten minutes later and saw once more the shadows caused by the weird nooks and crannies of the old house, I found myself shaking again. The thing I had seen on the attic back stairs might still be somewhere near. If I really had only imagined the dead woman, then what was to prevent my conjuring her up again? But if she was real, if Sybil Thursten had come back ... or had never died. ...

I shuddered and rushed downstairs, seeing no one, but running as if she were right at my heels.

I found everyone gathered in the lanai, finishing what proved to be second or third Mai-tais all around. Mai-tais always filled me up as if I'd eaten a large bowl of heavily spiked fruit, so when Mark came to the doorway and led me to the couch, I refused Dion Bates' flippant offer of the Mai-tai that he had been making for himself.

"No. Don't bother," Mark said impatiently. "She was sick all morning, and we want her to have an appetite for dinner."

I smiled at him, trying to show my gratitude for his care of me, even if it was of a fatherly kind. Then, as I turned to refuse again the drink in Dion Bates' hands, I saw his eyes. They were far from laughing, far from mocking or flippant. In their depths I thought I read concern for me. Or was it only curiosity? I was torn between uneasiness and the prickling hope that he was only what he said he was, and not the "psycho" Joe Nakazawa thought him.

Carol Jeffrey, her delicate face well made up for a change, was making small talk with Bobbie, who kept staring at her father. It was not the accusing look that must have haunted him during the trial, but it was thoughtful, and disconcerting for that very reason. I knew it made Mark suffer, because he looked pale now, and troubled. There were many strange currents throughout the room. Mrs. Jeffrey, sitting there elegantly sipping a Gin Sling, was watching her granddaughter over the rim of her glass, her eyes as opaque and unreadable as the frosted glass. I wondered if, in some sinister way, she was projecting her thoughts to Bobbie, feeding the girl suspicions of her father. If so, it was worse than cruel. It was vicious and insane.

Now Dion Bates was talking to Mark, discussing the age of the house, its history, the Thursten sea captain who had come here with Mrs. Tomei's grandfather. I watched Mark's tired face brighten to enthusiasm; when we were called in to dinner, the two men were still talking. The subject was trivial. This time they joined in condemning the rapid commercialization of the Haleiwa District. But I was enormously relieved. I wanted Mark to stop dwelling on the immediate past, and above all, I wanted him to begin to enjoy life again. As a kind of offshoot of this passionate wish, I began for the first time to admire Dion Bates genuinely.

It was all very well for me to try to dismiss as imaginary my chilling encounter with the "ghost" of Sybil Thursten this afternoon, but I

160

felt a trifle more secure with Dion Bates among us. I reasoned that if he were guilty of the recent horrors here, he wouldn't be behaving so well tonight, making what seemed such genuine efforts at getting everyone to relax.

Dinner, on the surface, was a calm, pleasant success. It was only when the meal ended, and coffee was served, that I realized I had been lulled into a false security.

Mrs. Jeffrey, speaking for the first time since dinner began, announced to all of us: "Our physical needs seem to be satisfied. Shall we now change into comfortable clothes and then adjourn to the living room and the real business of the evening? The séance?"

It might have taken me longer to realize that I was indeed the scapegoat of the evening, their absurd mediumistic contact with the other side, if they hadn't all turned in their chairs to stare at me. Even Mark. And even Dion Bates, who had seemed, so recently, to be my friend.

Mark reached over and touched my hand sympathetically. "Are you all right, child?"

I jerked my hand away and started to get up, but everywhere there were eyes on me. I couldn't escape them. I looked at each face. It was amazing how anxious they were! Finally, there was Dion Bates. He looked particularly tense, but he asked me in a low voice, "Will you help us? We need you."

Fumbling a little, I pulled my chair forward

again and sat down slowly while I watched Bates.

"Wh—what do I have to do?"

They all began to perk up, to get excited and expectant. Everybody talked at once, trying to instruct me. At last Mark cut into the jumble of words in his authoritative way.

"Let Bates explain it. It's his department," and everyone subsided except the man I had once thought of as a death image. He explained that I had very little to do physically; I was just to sit in a chair at the table and help to work that silly Ouija board. I had a mental role to play, too, however. I was also supposed to make my mind a blank, which is a good deal harder than one might think. Then I was simply to let any thoughts come to me as they would, including, I knew, a possible contact from the other side by Sybil Thursten. The mere idea of being again visited from the grave by that creature with the mischievous light in her well-made-up eyes was horrifying. It had certainly been so on those servants' stairs a few hours ago. I didn't want to repeat the meeting.

But from the look of it, I wasn't going to be given any choice. Somehow I couldn't resist the combined anxiety of those people. After the women had changed clothes in accordance with Mrs. Jeffrey's dictum, we all adjourned to the shadowy living room where Bobbie's Ouija board had already been placed on a round walnut table. There were chairs for all of us, including Bobbie. I didn't approve of her being present; I felt that it was a cruel thing Mrs. Jeffrey was doing, and Mark too, to permit the girl to witness this hocus-pocus. If, in a ghastly moment, Bobbie's mother did in some way materialize, it would surely in no way reconcile Bobbie to her death. But we had all gone too far now to turn back. I was certain of that as I studied the spidery shadow of the three-legged pointer on the Ouija board.

Mrs. Jeffrey's insistence that we dress comfortably was based on the idea that no externals should interfere with our concentration on the eerie business ahead. Wearing my one pair of glamorous hostess pajamas, I wasn't surprised to note that the other women looked very nearly as silly as I felt myself to be. Carol, Mrs. Jeffrey, and even Bobbie wore tentlike North African djellabas, or maybe they were caftans, I wasn't sure, and the combination of red, orange, blue and purple was enough to blind a self-respecting ghost, even given Sybil Thursten's taste in clothes. Only the two men were dressed very much the same as usual.

I sat down in the chair pointed out to me, and surreptitiously felt around under it and under the table, wondering if someone might have rigged up wires or bells or "ectoplasm" to assist in the false raising of the dead woman. I found nothing, however, so I supposed that whoever was really the instigator of this séance would serve his or her own purposes in another way.

Mark and Bobbie set glasses of water around the table when, due to the spicy seasonings of our curried dinner, everyone proved to be thirsty, and when Bobbie had finished, she covered the Ouija board pointer with the palms of her hands. In spite of my private conviction that all of this séance business was a trick, I couldn't help being exceedingly curious about the results of Bobbie's little test. But she was nervous and impatient; when nothing happened after sixty seconds, she gave up.

Dion Bates, in his role as what he called flippantly "master of the revels," instructed us in the use of the Ouija board and stressed the importance of not wiping our nervous hands on our clothing. He seemed to have a theory that the perspiration of our palms would influence the movements of the pointer over the Ouija board.

All the lights in the living room were turned off, so that our only illumination was the faint glow from the low-burning fire in the fireplace, which emitted snap and crackle of pitch in the wood occasionally. It barely gave us enough light to make out the letters and numbers on the Ouija board.

Our seating arrangements were of great significance to me, because I was sure someone would try a trick, and if we weren't careful, we would believe anything we were intended to believe. Mark was seated at my right, and Mrs. Jeffrey at my left. I sipped water and strained my eyes to study the face at each place, wondering which of them would pull off the expected supernatural act. Beyond Mark was Carol. Then Bates, opposite me at the table, and then Bobbie. I was glad to have Mrs. Jeffrey next to me. It would be less easy for her to try any tricks.

By the time everyone was finally seated, I could almost believe Dion Bates had been right when he'd indicated that I would gradually come under the spell of the séance. While I should have been alert, sharp, and eying every movement suspiciously, I felt instead unnerved and distracted, caught under the spell of this strange business that pretended to connect the world of the dead with that of the, in some cases, vengeful living.

"Place your fingertips on the board," Bates told us, and we eventually got this done, though at first I was somewhat confused; I thought I was being instructed to touch the big lettered board itself. But then I understood that I was to put my fingertips on the pointer, and I did so. It seemed, to me, that if there were a very much embodied spirit of Sybil Thursten in the house, we were certainly providing her with ready-made headquarters. I couldn't tell what Bates was thinking. Half the time his gaze was fixed on me, whether protectively, curiously, or accusingly, I couldn't tell in the dim light. The two women were concentrating, staring at the Ouija board and Mark, frowning, was equally intent. But, like me, Bobbie looked around almost furtively, and I wondered if she too was trying to catch someone in a trick to torment the rest of us. From this idea I advanced to the thought that I would be much better off if I knew everything Bobbie Thursten must know.

I was thinking this and other vague, mixed thoughts when I realized, to my astonishment, that the light triangular piece of wood with three legs, the pointer, was moving under my fingertips without any impetus from me, or even from Mark or Mrs. Jeffrey. Only we three had our fingertips on the pointer at this moment.

"Look!" Bobbie whispered. "It's spelling. A . . . Ada? That's Grandma."

I glanced at Mrs. Jeffrey, whom I could not see clearly. Her brows seemed wrinkled, as if none of this made sense. A few seconds later, in spite of the concentration of the six of us, the pointer moved erratically from "A" to "3" and then to "X." All gibberish.

I was trying to concentrate, but it became more and more difficult. I found myself hypnotized by the roving pointer whose shadow stretched longer and longer as the fire in the fireplace died down, until it really looked like a gigantic black spider crawling across the board. And all the time it seemed to be moving entirely of its own volition.

"We must ask it questions," Dion Bates murmured softly. "Who begins?"

Startling me by the abrupt excitement in his voice, Mark cut in suddenly, "Sybil! Sybil! Can you hear us?"

Bobbie had put her fingertips on the Ouija board, then delicately transferred them to the pointer. Now she closed her eyes, almost echoing her father's words. "Mother? Are you with us? Please, let us know if you are."

I wondered if they all heard the same painful plea in the girl's voice that I did. At the same time that I was being lulled into a strange, half-somnambulist state, during which I found myself more aware than ever of the eerie currents around us, I had a growing anxiety to turn around. I felt that something terrible from another world hovered in that great dark behind us, that dark which had gradually engulfed us so that it was now hard to make out any of the faces around the table. Under an impulse beyond my own comprehension, I leaned closer to the board and murmured, "Is someone with us now?"

Though the dying fire left the room more and more in darkness, so that it was very difficult to read the board, when I looked up I imagined that eyes glittered everywhere around the table, eyes like cold, passionless stars. I confused Carol's eyes with Bobbie's and could scarcely see Bates' dark eyes at all. But these desultory thoughts abruptly ceased. The pointer was moving again. Somebody—I thought it was Bobbie—read aloud:

"Y . . . e . . ."

We all repeated the word "yes" in unison.

"Are you Sybil?" Mark asked in the same painful, longing voice as his daughter's.

Again the affirmative. I wondered for the first time if there wasn't a trifling pressure from someone else around the table, but I couldn't place the direction because of the erratic movements on the Ouija board.

"Sybil, how did you die?" Mrs. Jeffrey asked, so hoarsely that I didn't at once recognize her voice.

The room was so dark now that I had to squint to read the board at all. I wondered why no one got up to turn on a lamp or at least build up the fire. Again I felt outside pressures closing around us, in the obscurity of the long room. Was the dead woman creeping up on our defenseless backs at this precise second? Nothing was visible on the table except various fingers, pale and indistinct. I wasn't sure whose feminine hand I felt at one time. The long, graceful fingers rode gently on the pointer beside my own. The touch of the strange fingers was like smooth ice, and in panic I drew my hand back, but no one else seemed to share my revulsion. Other fingers took the place of my own, and I closed my eyes momentarily, hoping that when I opened them I could identify each of those blurred and now sinister faces.

But they began to show a confusing similarity. I could hardly tell one from the other, save by voice. Someone else was suffering as I was. Mark protested in a hoarse whisper, "You are moving it! Take your hand from it!"

Bobbie's voice, plaintive and pitiful, haunted me long after that night. "Mother? Are you here with us? Please! Let us know. Say something."

I started to lean forward, to identify as best I could the faces around the table. I was trying to verify a ghastly suspicion that people were not where they should be. Perhaps a *dead* hand was guiding the pointer.

"Quiet! It's moving!" Dion Bates commanded sharply.

Someone I couldn't identify spelled out in a heavy whisper, "I . . . A . . . M . . . H . . . E . . ."

"I'm here," Bobbie translated, and added again, "Mother?"

Bates said, "Hush!"

The pointer began its idiotic yet uncanny journeying, and I watched the confusing letters and numbers, not at all sure what message was being spelled out.

"M...U...R...D...E...R..."

I felt an hysterical desire to laugh, but the spelling repeated itself, this time less likely to make me laugh:

"E...D...M...U...R...D..."

"Murdered!" Mrs. Jeffrey's voice sounded strangely weak, breathy and old. "Sybil—who?"

I felt the severe chill of the scene, and of the house itself. The fire had burned too low to offer any warmth and when sparks snapped and spurted upward from the pitch burning, several of us jumped. A moment later the blackened log dropped into ashes and the room was completely dark. Lights outside the room had gone out too. Someone gasped, and I heard heavy breathing near me.

"The lamp lights, damn it!" Mark called impatiently, making his stumbling passage across the room. He was followed by others. I could hear people stumbling frantically about, banging up against furniture and walls. In the distance a door slammed. Everyone was moving, it seemed, except me. For one thing, I was too unfamiliar with the room, and for another, I was mortally afraid of meeting the creature I had seen earlier this evening on the attic stairs.

I could hardly believe we had returned to normal when the long room, strewn with overturned furniture, was at last illuminated fitfully by a small ceiling light in the hall. The party had scattered. Mark was examining a lamp cord by the card table in the corner. The cord had obviously been pulled out from the wall, perhaps tripped by someone's foot in the darkness following the séance. Bobbie was staring bewilderedly across the table. She seemed to be staring at me, but then I looked to my left and saw that Mrs. Jeffrey had fallen forward over the table with her cheek against the tabletop and one hand extended toward the Ouija board. Everyone spoke at once, including Bates, who was at the fireplace holding up a piece of faint-glowing firewood between the tongs. I wondered if he expected to illuminate the scene with it or what other reason had brought him to that spot. I leaned over Mrs. Jeffrey, putting the back of my hand to the dry flesh of her exposed cheek. It felt chilled, but I was enormously relieved when I saw that she was breathing.

"She seems to have fainted," I said, and watched each of them to read any betraying anger or fear. I was suspicious of them all. But none of them, not Bobbie, Mark, or Dion Bates, showed anything other than the same relief that I was feeling.

"Mrs. Jeffrey," I said, speaking as calmly as I could, "can you hear me?" Bobbie gave me the only glass of water that hadn't been tipped over during the panicky upheaval in the dark, and after a few sips the old lady opened her eyes.

"Sybil?" she whispered, her pale eyes staring glassily around the room. "Tell Carol—I saw her...."

For the first time since we had discovered that Mrs. Jeffrey was not seriously hurt, we looked at each other, sharing the same tension, the same hideous doubt. Bobbie voiced it in a high-pitched, frightened question.

"Where are you? Aunt Carol...?"

Twelve

We all seemed unduly panicked over a matter that on the surface was of slight importance. Carol had undoubtedly left the room to find candles, a flashlight. She might even—for I remembered the slamming door—be outside, looking for a lantern.

"Where the devil has the girl gone?" Mark asked no one in particular as he looked out into the hall, first toward the lanai and then toward Mrs. Tomei's little apartment next to the kitchen. "I'll check upstairs. Bobbie, will you help me?"

When they were gone I started to get up, but found myself surprisingly weak and shaken. Strong hands tightened under my arms to pull me up and I looked around, scowling at Dion Bates.

"It's your fault—the whole stupid séance!" I reminded him, but when I saw his eyes, their flickering uncertainty and anxiety, I was sorry I had brought up this unpleasant truth. He was

173

being gentle and kind, and I appreciated it. I had never known a man whose actions seemed more sinister; yet I was drawn to him in a way, especially physical, that I had not experienced with my older and more mature idol, Mark.

Dion was about to say something to me, something sympathetic to judge from the look on his face, when Bobbie's terror-filled voice rang through the upper quarters of the old house. "Aunt Carol? Where are you?"

Her fright was contagious. I murmured shakily to Dion, "It's *got* to be something slight. Some idea Carol had about ... what happened. Or maybe she was frightened away by something at the séance. It was enough to scare anybody!"

"Possibly," Dion said, but there was doubt here, nothing like the quick, charmingly confident air I had mistrusted in the man until now. Odd, I thought, that I should for the first time feel free to trust this man whose fascination from the first had not escaped me. The irony was that the less sure, the less clever he proved himself, the freer I felt to trust him.

Mark had evidently instructed Mrs. Tomei by this time, for the little cook came shakily through the flickering lights and shadows of the living room to sit beside Mrs. Jeffrey and murmur to her soothingly. She explained to us in a low voice that she would take "poor lady to her bed." I thought all this very good of Mrs. Tomei; I didn't envy her the job. Mrs. Jeffrey looked dazed and gray and aching with fear. She clutched the cook's sleeves and kept murmuring confusedly, "She will come back. It was not meant, you know. Not this way—"

I said hurriedly, "Her daughter can't have gone far. But the longer we wait, the further she'll get maybe, unless she really has only gone to find a light." By this time, though, it was clear that none of us believed that.

"I only wish that were the—" Dion began, then cut off this curious wish and rushed me out of the room and along the hall to the lanai. The lights came on immediately when we tried them. Whoever had turned off those outside lights and thus ended the séance was entirely human. We left the lanai lamps on as we hurried out, down the steps that had presumably killed Sybil Thursten, and across the sand.

It was a strange night, outside as well as inside the Beach House. The sky still had a vaguely pink cast toward the east, although it was well on in the night. There was a wind, snappish along the beach, blowing sand in desertlike swirls and eddies. I yelled suddenly, "Don't forget the *imu*! It's somewhere out there."

Dion Bates stopped abruptly and looked at me. Even in the half dark I read the warmth in his dark eyes. Whether the warmth was due to gratitude that I should care whether he broke his neck or not, I couldn't tell. But it was there. Disturbed as I was about Carol's curious disappearance, I nevertheless couldn't help feeling a sudden stirring of happiness. There was no denying that Dion Bates had become a central figure in my thoughts. Even my girlish crush on my employer was beginning to move back into proper perspective, and I saw it clearly for what it had been—hero worship of an older and dominating male.

"Thank you," Dion said. "You needn't have warned me, you know. I don't deserve it, after the other day."

As we made our way with care along the beach toward the west side of the house, where the wind died down to a mere tropic whisper, I asked, "Did you let me fall in that hole the other day? I could have broken my leg. Or my neck."

His admission staggered me. "I know. Though the neck part would have been most unlikely." But the honesty of this put me off my guard too.

"Well, can't you tell me why it—" I began, and was rudely cut off.

"No, not yet. ... This way. We'll try toward the road and meet Thursten and his daughter out back."

The moon helped us, though it kept dodging in and out, as if this were a kind of hide-and-seek game instead of what now threatened to be a deadly search. I looked around suddenly, overcome by a bad case of jitters. . . . Why, even mentally, had I called this a deadly search? But Carol had chosen those moments of eerie dark at the séance to run away, stirring us all to this frenzy of search and worry.

"Why do you think she did it?" I asked Bates, while breathlessly climbing the little slope after him to the road above.

He looked at me as if I had said something totally incomprehensible, in another language.

"What do you mean—'she did it'?" Then he seemed to remember something, inhaled sharply, and after an odd little pause, shrugged. "Haven't the faintest. Here. Let me give you a hand up."

We saw a shadowy figure stalking across the brief diamond pattern of light on the road and I held back. But someone recognized better than I did Mark's lean, sinewy form. His daughter called to him from the direction of the kitchen entry and went to him as he held out his arms to her. It was good to watch, especially as she called him "Father" for the first time I could remember since her mother's death.

"Have you seen any sign of her?" I asked, as we joined forces near the half-finished garage.

Mark was shaking a large flashlight which didn't work, but it made a handy weapon, though I couldn't imagine why he'd need one.

"I'm beginning to think she may have started back toward the village," he remarked, staring over his daughter's head into the thick jungle growth south of the road. He added thoughtfully, "At any rate, I hope to God that's what she did."

For one split second I was aware of a thing so unexpected, I felt that nothing at the séance had been as horrible. It was the quick, sidewise exchange of knowing glances between Dion Bates and Mark's daughter. And it occurred at precisely the second when Mark suggested that Carol might have started toward the village. In spite of all the ups and downs in my suspicions lately, I had at last begun to trust Dion Bates. This curious and, to me, sinister exchange between them erased that trust as well as my sympathy with young Bobbie. I looked around and asked about the lighting on this road; it was appallingly ill-lighted.

Mark agreed grimly. "We've complained about it often enough. Sybil used to say—" He broke off. "Carol has her little car parked beyond the garage; she had someone drive it out here for her yesterday. It's over here somewhere."

"How is Mrs. Jeffrey?" Bates asked, stopping Mark and me abruptly as we made our way through the dark beside the high stack of lumber left by Joe Nakazawa and his friend.

"Mrs. Tomei is with her," Mark reassured

him and motioned to his daughter to join us. But Bobbie did not seem to see him. She began to beat the leafy brush angrily with a board she had taken from the heap by the garage. I saw that Carol's car was still where it had been parked the day before, and then I glanced at Bobbie. It worried me that Bates joined her now, though he merely pushed aside a gnarled bush with one hand and then surreptitiously shook his head. What *was* this between him and Bobbie?

They began to move in the direction of town; they did nothing more that seemed significant to me and I gave them up, going along with Mark, who looked terribly grim as he examined the car.

"Nothing in it. No signs," he said to me rather tensely. It was bad enough with everyone else obviously fearing the worst, but when my staunch and sturdy oak, Mark Thursten, began to crumple, it was as if the stars had fallen out of the sky.

"What does that mean? Is it bad?" I hoped he would lie. I was frightened enough without having further fears confirmed out here in the somber night.

He completed his inspection, handing me the useless flashlight while he looked hard into the car through the windows. "No. Even with lights, I doubt if we would find anything."

"What are you looking for?" Then, as I was

179

somehow afraid of what he might tell me, I added hurriedly, "I mean—some clue, or something?"

"I don't know myself. That damned flash. . . . Well, no matter. What are they up to?"

"Who? Oh." I squinted into the moonlight and the endless sprays of darkness along the road. Bobbie was still close at hand, staunchly but ineffectually beating back the bushes. "Your daughter is right here. Mr. Bates is further along. He has one of those little round electronic lights he's carrying in the palm of his hand."

Mark moved away from the car, took my arm, and called to Bobbie. "Barbara, you had better run along in now. Your grandmother may need you."

Very pale in the moonlight, Bobbie looked around at us, making vague wide gestures. "Father, she must have left some sign. She must have! Even footprints—if she was on her feet."

I wondered at her concern now, considering that strange common bond I had surprised between her and Bates only minutes before. But her father, obviously worried about her wandering off in the cool, salt-rimed darkness that had swallowed up her aunt, said sternly, "Go back to the house, Bobbie. Please. Why don't you check off Aunt Carol's coats and jackets? See if you can find one missing. That will be a big help."

The girl hesitated. This time she made no attempt to look at Dion Bates, who was much further down the road, half hidden by an ancient, twisted *hau* tree.

"You may be right, Daddy. I'll check on her coats and stuff," and abruptly, she began to make great strides down the slope to the kitchen entryway of the Beach House. Puzzled and terribly uneasy as I was over her odd bond with Bates, I was still relieved that the scarring effect of her mother's death and the obvious malign influence of the Jeffreys had begun to wear off. Mark was her "daddy" again. I wondered, as she vanished inside the house, if the events of the séance and Carol's disappearance had anything to do with Bobbie's renewed kindness to her father. Whatever the cause, I was glad for Mark.

His stern face had scarcely relaxed, however. He said to me, "Until we hear anything from Barbara, I had better keep looking for footprints, since she hasn't taken her car. Come along. I'll find another flash. This thing is certainly useless."

I said quickly, in a low voice, "Let me wait for you here. I want to see what Bates is up to."

Mark glanced toward Mrs. Tomei's "death image" speculatively. "Yes. You may be right. I wonder if he had any foreknowledge of—" He must have noticed me looking all around at the hovering dark, because he broke off. "Well, we'll find out. Try and stay in that patch of moonlight. Then I can keep you in sight. Just in case—"

"Never mind," I interrupted hastily. "Don't explain that."

That made him smile, but I could imagine the effort it took to do so. I walked rapidly toward the moonlight he had pointed out, and as this was also in the direction taken by Dion Bates, I was surprised and even more upset to discover he had by this time vanished among the shadows and the wild, tropic foliage that encroached on the sandy south shoulder of the road. I had no intention of going after him alone and perhaps being led into some kind of trap among the unknown plant and animal life of that labyrinth, but as I studied it, I realized it would be hardly possible to become lost, or even—heaven forbid!—to hide a body among those bushes. The fields were just beyond, and within a matter of hours whatever was hidden there would be found. Mark had gone into the house by this time and turned on the kitchen lights. I did want to do my best to keep tabs on Bates' nocturnal prowling, but at the same time, I wondered what Bobbie had found in the missing woman's room. Or rather, as I hoped, what she had not found in the way of coats or jackets.

I thought I made out among the great tropic leaves certain flashes from that light Bates held in his palm, but it was hard to tell. The clouds overhead were scudding so fast across the face of the moon that the immediate vicinity was almost flashing with light and dark. I moved very slowly, attempting to keep within the light, while I traced what looked like Bates' mysterious progress through the little jungle grove to the fields beyond. Why on earth was he wandering through these almost inaccessible plants? I couldn't think of any reason why Carol Jeffrey should either be hiding there or be hidden there by her murderer. It would be an impossible job, carrying or dragging a body into that tangle so quickly, and even if accomplished, would surely leave tracks of some kind at the point of entry.

Her murderer? It was the first time since the séance I had admitted seriously that murder was uppermost on my mind. I pulled my thin jacket closer around me. Up here, slightly sheltered by the house, the night air held the perfumed warmth I associated with Hawaii, but my skin prickled. Mark appeared at a kitchen window and waved something at me. I assumed it was another flashlight and nodded, waiting for him to join me, but by this time Bates had entirely disappeared.

So much the worse for him, I told myself. If he wanted to fool around getting lost in our local jungle, that was his problem. I went down the slope to meet Mark. He was smiling and looked younger, as relieved as I was when he called to Bobbie, "Come in the kitchen, dear. Tell Livia what you discovered."

The girl took a few minutes to join us, explaining, "We've got Grandma settled now. I think she'll sleep tonight."

"Yes, but tell about your Aunt Carol."

"Oh. Sure." Her tired eyes wandered to me. She seemed a trifle less worried than she had been, but the effects of this weird night had left their marks on her. She looked quite mature. A pity she had to grow up this way. "Aunt Carol's gone into town. She must have walked."

I looked at both of them, wondering how they could be so sure. Mark put a hand on Bobbie's shoulder and she did not make her usual shrinking gesture. He explained, "Carol always wears the same things to the village when she walks. An old padded coolie coat and some white plastic boots. They're both gone." His fingers tightened briefly, comfortingly on his daughter's shoulder, then he let her go with a fatherly, almost playful little push, a gesture I hadn't seen him make since Sybil Thursten died. It was plain that he, at least, felt his relationship with Bobbie was improving. I wished I could be as sure of the girl. "Run along with Livia and get some sleep. It's been a very long day."

"But Aunt Carol!" the girl protested, as she and I were starting out of the room.

"I promise. I'll take your friend Bates and we'll scour the road and the village. We'll bring Aunt Carol back. How's that?"

She finally agreed and went up the dark back stairs with me. The lights were on in the upper hall, for which I was grateful. I felt as tired as Bobbie looked and I must have looked twenty years older myself. Every bone seemed to hurt, and since I had actually done very little physically, I could trace my sick tiredness to the emotional shock of the terrors we had all undergone. Nor was the night over yet. I yawned and shivered.

"I'll say good night, Bobbie. I'm exhausted. I imagine you are, too." As she hesitated, obviously still upset, I felt reasonably confident enough about Carol Jeffrey to assure her, "With your father and Mr. Bates both going into town after her, your aunt will be back here in no time."

"Will she?" the girl asked bleakly. "Look! Would you come out on Mother's lanai with me? I want to watch Daddy meet Mr. Bates."

It was such an unexpected request that I suspected there must be trickery somewhere. I said nothing but walked down the hall with her toward the beach front of the house. She looked quickly at her mother's bedroom door and I thought she was going to expect me to reach the small lanai through that haunted white suite. Though she went so far as to put

185

her hand on the elegant door latch, she must have seen something in my face that warned her. She slid her fingers off the latch and we went instead to the hall door.

In the lanai I slid open a window. The night world of beach and rolling sea waves was edged with silver where the moon was visible, and had a deceptively soft look like midnight-blue velvet beyond the silver periphery.

"There!" Bobbie exclaimed, pointing to where the road wound away into the dark. "That's Daddy's car. Let's see if he stops."

Before stopping, he drove almost beyond the patches of moonlight, and only the red tail lights clued us in on his exact position.

"He's stopped!" I was happy to assure her. "He must have found Bates."

We could see the slim dark figure of Dion Bates pass in front of the car lights. Then he got in beside Mark and they drove on. We watched the tail lights of the car until it disappeared beyond a jutting headland close to the village.

"Okay," Bobbie agreed finally, with a big, tired sigh. "They're safe now. If she's there, they'll find her, between them. Let's go to bed." With shaking hands she slid the window shut and we went back into the hall. "Funny," Bobbie murmured, blinking at the sudden brightness. "Sometimes it's even worse with the lights on."

She was right. As we separated and went into our own bedrooms, I was glad enough to get away from the brilliance of the hall's overhead lights plus the two lamps on the tables at either end of the hall. Whether it was the inappropriateness of all this illumination at such a late hour, or whether it was just that none of us trusted anyone else's face after all that had happened, I couldn't be sure, but I shared Bobbie's feeling.

I turned on the lamp by my bed, grateful for the soft glow, and without giving myself more than a haphazard washing up I jumped into bed, aware all over again that my body felt as if it had been beaten and trampled on. I was still so nervous I thought nothing would make me sleep, but ten minutes after I hit the bed I was dreaming—ghastly, tangled things about séances and a dead Sybil Thursten somewhere very much alive, and other, even greater horrors, all in shadow. Eyes gleamed again around a badly lighted Ouija board, and the fingers that rode the spidery dark pointer were fingers of the dead.

Voices in the hall brought me tensely out of this morass of the supernatural, for which I was momentarily grateful. I glanced at the illuminated dial of my little travel clock. It was 1:40 A.M., and Bobbie was speaking with shrill force, considering the hour.

"But Daddy! She must have been somewhere along the road. Or in town."

Mark said something slowly and tiredly which was not quite audible, and then Bobbie came back with the fierce accusation, "Then you missed her. Aunt Carol has to be somewhere. She just has to! What did Mr. Bates say?"

This time Mark lost what remained of his patience. "*Mr. Bates* was with me the entire time. If we couldn't find her, you may as well let him share the blame."

"But where is he now?"

"Home in his bed, I devoutly trust!" Mark said acidly. "I certainly don't want him prowling around here in the dead of night."

"Oh, Daddy, don't be so silly! What could he do to us?"

"For God's sake, Barbara, good night! Go back to bed."

After that they went their separate ways and two doors slammed. I pitied them both, wondering if, after all, a wedge had been driven so deeply between them that they would never be able to overcome the ugly barrier of Sybil Thursten's death.

It was hard to sleep now. My first painful need for rest had been satisfied, the edge of fatigue blunted as on that first night, and I sat up stiffly in bed listening, without being at all sure what I expect to hear. When nothing happened after half an hour, which passed rapidly yet vaguely, I found that my head was propped against the wall and that I was beginning to yawn.

"Good!" I thought. "Maybe now I can get back to a decent half night's sleep."

I lay down and closed my eyes. My nerves crossed me up by jumping, first in my left eye and then in my throat. I debated whether this was actually a nerve or a pulse, hoping the subject would put me to sleep again.

Perhaps I dozed off, though I have a recollection of the passage of time, but shortly after 2:30 I heard a peculiar noise somewhere in the house, a dull, heavy sound, a thump. Considering what the whole household had been through, I wondered that everyone didn't wake up on the instant and plow downstairs to find the source of the racket. On the other hand, I couldn't imagine any member of the household being energetic enough at this hour of the night to be moving furniture with a thump like that: a second thump came along while I wondered what had caused the first betraying sound.

I sat up, pushed my arms into the sleeves of a wholly inadequate blue nylon peignoir, and made my way to my bedroom door. I had no more intention of going down to identify those sounds than of swimming the Pacific. Nevertheless, in view of Carol's disappearance earlier in the evening, and of Mark and Bates' empty-handed return from the village, I had very little doubt that Carol was coming back now, and would make some noble and defensive claim tomorrow. The more I thought of her trick, the more I hoped Mark would order her out of the house tomorrow and stop being troubled by the idiotic accusations of the Jeffrey females. I was now seriously considering an abrupt departure myself, after tonight's doings.

I opened the door an inch or two and sneaked a quick glance at the deserted hall. Someone, probably Mark, who was the last through the hall, had turned out all but a tiny night light by the lanai door. This time, suddenly, there was no mistaking the slam of a door downstairs.

She really did have a colossal nerve. Everyone else in the household was here, so this had to be Carol. ... Unless, of course, it was Dion Bates, sneaking back into the house after Mark had left him at his own apartment, wherever that was. It was sickening about Bates, sickening that I couldn't banish him from my thoughts. He still attracted me in a devastating way; yet I could be quite capable of suspecting him of any crime. It was past understanding. It seemed unlikely that he was sneaking back, though. If Dion prowled around the Beach House, he would hardly make all this racket. I stepped out into the hall, then set one bare foot on a raised tack in the carpet and retreated angrily, resentful alike of the tack, the worn carpet, and my own clumsiness. As I slipped my feet into flat-soled mules, I added Miss Carol Jeffrey to my list of grievances.

What the devil *was* she doing banging around at this ungodly hour?

I ventured out into the hall again, saw and heard nothing in the lean, slanting shadows cast by the hall's meager furnishings. I made up my mind that nothing would get me to leave the stairs, but from the vantage point of the lowest stair I would be able to see most of the living room, the greater part of the lanai, and all of the hall. I went down slowly, remembering more or less at the back of my mind that it had been on a staircase that I had seen Sybil Thursten or her double.

There was no ghost, no double, on these stairs. But one small light was glowing in the living room. Reminding myself that I wasn't going to wander around getting my head bashed in, or otherwise interfering with whatever Carol had in mind, I peeked around the open door and got a full view of the living room.

Exactly what I had expected: Carol Jeffrey was sitting at the table in the far end of the room. The Ouija board remained where we had left it. The pointer was on its side. Her hand, white and clammy in the faint light, was outstretched on the table, nearly touching the pointer. Amazing how much she resembled her dead sister, Sybil! And even more surprising that I had never noticed this resemblance so markedly before. Probably it *was* her makeup. She usually wore so little. She was staring at the Ouija board, and her fine-spun dark gold hair, usually so neat, so proper, was dishevelled, with uneven tendrils concealing her forehead.

I called out angrily from the doorway: "Miss Jeffrey! If you must wander around the house at three A.M., please don't make so much noise about it."

Carol did not look up at me. After a few puzzled seconds, I had a feeling she hadn't even heard me.

"Miss Jeffrey?" I repeated with less assurance. This time I slipped into the room, still staring at her. The resemblance to the dead Sybil Thursten was even more pronounced as I approached her and I stopped halfway around the table, numbed by the possibility that this motionless, staring creature, pale as the dead, was not Carol at all. Not trusting myself to speak again, I managed to reach out a hand across the Ouija board, my fingers groping shakily for hers. It was not the stiffened fingers that told me the truth, but the pale-eyed stare. . . . Was this Carol? Or was it Sybil Thursten?

It no longer mattered. Whoever she was, the woman was dead.

Thirteen

I stumbled over the chair Dion Bates had used during the séance, and fell into the cushioned seat on my knees. During those seconds I remember, amid the confusion of my mind, the hope that when I swung around laboriously to stare at the head of the table, I would see nothing at all except an empty chair.

But she was still there, hideously propped up in that chair, though she had obviously been dead for hours. Even I, with my limited experience, could tell that. I was too weak to examine her, too weak to move, although I tried again to get to my feet, and failed. The world, at least my little section of it at Beach House, whirled around before my eyes, even behind closed lids, and I thought I was going to be sick. I swallowed rapidly several times.

A hand touched my shoulder and this time I managed to cry out, a strangled sound, but I was too terrified to do more. I didn't know what I expected to see, certainly not Dion

Bates, who was looking down at me, his face in shadows but his voice edged with that sympathy and concern I had surprised in him earlier in the evening, when we first went to search for Carol.

"Don't, Livy! You shouldn't have seen this. It wasn't meant for you."

"Thank you. That makes—all the difference." I had a hard time croaking out the ironic words. I was frozen by the horror of this thing and couldn't seem to get hold of myself.

"Please, Livy ... please don't be frightened. I wouldn't hurt you for anything."

I was still stupefied, and dangerously trustful as he kissed my cold cheek gently and helped me off the chair.

"Come. We've got to be quick. It has to be done. I wish to God it didn't." He was leading me past that dreadful thing in the chair when he stopped and shook me suddenly, with his hands on both my shoulders. He looked into my eyes. His own seemed to burn with a dark fire, like coals ignited by a breath of air.

"You are just the one. Will you do it, darling? Will you sit here where she is? Will you do this for poor Carol? For all of us? Otherwise, her body will fall any minute. And the whole plan with it."

As he drew me near the dead woman, I protested in panic, "No, no! I won't!" But I did. I didn't understand his plan or why he listened for a minute, glancing tensely at the doorway into the hall. Then he took my hair, already tousled, rearranged it over my forehead, and gently removed from the dead woman's shoulders Sybil Thursten's Siamese stole with its sparkling green and gold threads. I felt the material gathered about my own shoulders, the rough silk threads prickling through my peignoir. He stopped and listened once more; then, while I gasped, he lifted the dead Carol Jeffrey and carried her to the couch facing the fireplace.

I understood now what was expected of me, at least in part, and sat down as the dead woman had been seated, trying to put my hand out toward the pointer on the Ouija board, staring at the far end of the table but barely allowing myself to see whatever, or whoever, Dion expected to enter the living room from the hall. He came back immediately, hugged my chill, stiff shoulders, and whispered, "Don't worry, and don't say a word. No matter what you see. Remember! Not a word. You are perfectly safe. I'll be in the corner behind the buttress there." He kissed me on the crown of my head, a gesture I was not in a position or mood to appreciate, and was silently gone. The first new terror swept over me when the dim light was snapped off; magically, the room now held the flickering illumination of the fire that had been renewed in the fireplace.

I didn't know what to expect, or why I should trust Dion Bates, the death image, of all people, but I guessed that whatever we all feared was about to make its appearance, and only the presence of Bates himself, strangely, made the terror endurable. When the waiting got on my nerves again, I tried not to move but did let my veiled gaze flick over the area in the room where I hoped Bates was concealed. Coming out of my passive submission to his authority, I began to wonder whether Bates himself was the danger point. It was impossible to see him in his hiding place. Was he even there? He could be anywhere in the darkness behind me, or across the room, near the doorway into the hall. I heard a sound out in the hall, another loud thump such as had brought me downstairs in the first place.

This time, after sixty seconds or so, I heard footsteps on the stairs. I stiffened, not knowing the precise danger but instinctively afraid that this horrible charade was being acted out for the benefit of the unseen creature on the stairs. If I screamed now, or got up and exposed myself, I might, by this very move, bring on my own murder. I had only Dion Bates' word, and his actions—suspicious enough—to rely on.

The remnants of the fire fell apart, giving a spurt of light and then darkness. I started to get up, but stopped as the floorboards in the hall creaked and at the same time I saw strange

196

little circles of brightness. A flashlight. Suddenly, the faint circle of light focused on me. Fortunately, I remained in the position in which I had seen the dead woman. My face was partially concealed, and the Thai stole around my shoulders and my hair—its color, its dishevellment, the wisps crawling down over my forehead—all must have given the illusion of the dead woman.

I could see nothing beyond that circle of light, and for a few seconds even the angry, deadly whisper behind the light was unknown to me. The light traveled through the long room with the voice. I remained fixed in position, wondering if the heavy beat of my heart was evident.

"What is this, Carol? Another masquerade of yours? Wasn't it enough to hound me as Sybil? You think I didn't guess? You think there could ever be anyone like Sybil? She drove me to hit her. Taunted me with lies about our child. You really think I wanted her dead? The one person I have loved in my life?"

Dear God! Not Mark. . . .

My hand shook with a life of its own, and I stared down at it reflected in the shiny surface of the Ouija board. Vaguely, Mark's lean, strong figure was silhouetted behind the flashlight. I kept looking down, trying with every ounce of willpower not to show my sick disillusionment, which was greater than my fear.

Mark. . . . Mark. . . .

He never loved anyone but Sybil. I must always have known that. Strange that I had tried to fool myself for so long. But how could he kill his wife at the same time that he was in the office giving me my birthday present?

Soon he would be near enough to touch me. I couldn't believe he would hurt me. He had been the hero of too many of my daydreams. To my intense relief he raised the flash, taking the light off me. "Tell me, Carol, how did you get out of my study? You seemed dead enough when I put you there. . . . But it appears you weren't. What happened? How many times must you die?"

The flashlight was suddenly an instrument of violence. I still couldn't believe it. Not from Mark. I raised my head, but I didn't even put up a hand to ward off the blow. I still couldn't believe he would do it to me. The weapon was hard driven, the flashlight within inches of my forehead, when everything happened at once. The shadowy room seemed alive with people, though there were only two beside Mark and me. I heard several sickening blows struck, and Mark's body crashed against me, the flashlight arcing over my head and striking the carpet. Dion Bates dragged me out from under Mark's unconscious body, and I found myself looking into the calm black-olive eyes of the detective, Mr. Padilla.

I pressed my palms against my head. "It isn't happening," I said wildly. "He couldn't. He loved his wife. Terribly."

"I'm afraid that's why she died," Dion explained, looking at me with a care and warmth that went some way toward calming me. "I knew Sybil after Vietnam, when she came to help out at the hospital. My eyes were on the fritz. A shell fragment near the optic nerve. And Sybil used to read to us patients. She never got involved. Nothing like that. Just a bright, decent woman, a little flighty, maybe, but trying to help out."

"And I hated her," I murmured, terribly aware of the jealousy that had always distorted my view of Sybil Thursten. I looked up. "Did he mean to kill her?"

Mr. Padilla shook his big head in a ponderous, thoughtful way. "I think, from the fear of him that Mrs. Thursten expressed to this young man when they met again—"

"We met by accident."

"When they met on the beach one afternoon," Mr. Padilla went on, unflustered, "we must believe her death came as the result of a quarrel. She threatened to leave Thursten because of his uncontrollable jealousy and possessiveness. When he insisted he would get custody of their daughter Mrs. Thursten said the first thing that came into her mind. She denied his paternity."

Belatedly, I remembered that terrible truth. Poor Bobbie! "Good God! That's exactly what his daughter heard, and testified to."

Dion said, "Now you know why, when the verdict went in his favor, Bobbie and Sybil's family and I, too, believed you were in it together, that you had deliberately faked his alibi because you wanted to marry him."

"Did Mrs. Thursten think I was trying to make a play for her husband?" I asked with a good deal of bitterness. "When did she tell you about her fear of Mark?"

"The morning of the day she died. And she did not tell me of any suspicions about you."

Well, that was that! It was only hours after she expressed her fear of Mark that she was dead. No wonder Dion and the others had been so sure of his guilt! I looked up at the detective. "But I didn't fake Mark's alibi, Mr. Padilla. Honestly."

He nodded, but it was the way Dion squeezed my hand and smiled at me in his winning way that gave me courage. "There was a trick some way. It will work itself out," he assured me.

Although I wondered if I would ever sleep again after the horrors I had undergone at Beach House, I was glad enough to be taken to my room by Dion when the police arrived. I didn't want to see them arrest poor Mark, and I

200

didn't want to see them remove Carol Jeffrey's body.

"How did he kill Carol? And why did he do it?" I asked Dion as I sat on my bed feeling all the guilt of having, if inadvertently, shielded a killer, making it possible for him to kill again.

"Carol's frontal bone was cracked. A single heavy blow across the forehead would do it. It was just such a blow that killed his wife." Dion paused. "I think Thursten was angry and afraid right from the start about holding that séance. He suspected that the Jeffreys were going to rig it to accuse him of Sybil's murder with some kind of phony materialization of Sybil; at the same time, he half believed in spiritualism and he was afraid that Sybil really might appear. But if he refused to let the séance be held, it would look as if he were afraid of what Sybil would say if she came back. He must have been half out of his mind with guilt and fear and anger." Dion paused again. "Poor Carol," he said quietly. "She never even got the chance to make her appearance as Sybil, which was to be the climax of the séance. When she started manipulating the Ouija board to accuse Thursten of murder, that rage of his got the better of him, and she had to die. He may even have thought he was killing Sybil all over again. . . . I'm still not entirely convinced he didn't intend murder when he struck his wife. But we should never have allowed Carol to carry out the masquerade, in spite of her insistence. We should have realized that in Mark's condition anything could happen. As it did, in fact. The damned quick way he reacted in the dark!"

"Then Carol's body must have been locked in the study all the time we were searching for her outside?" Why this made it more horrible I did not know.

"There seems to be no doubt about it. He couldn't dispose of her until he was sure he wouldn't be interrupted. You see, he couldn't be sure no more of us were in the masquerade, and he had to be careful in ... burying her. Or whatever his plan might have been. At any rate, the study is where Padilla and I found her, some minutes before you came down and surprised us. We were setting up this macabre business to trap Thursten."

"It worked." I went on slowly, "It must have been ghastly for Mark when he saw he'd killed Sybil. And his own child overhearing most of their quarrel. And then the trial."

"Save a little sympathy for Miss Jeffrey. It wasn't Carol who poisoned the coffee, you know. Or who caused you the trouble with that *imu*. That was the old lady's idea. God knows how she did it." He looked at me and brushed hair out of my eyes with a gentle, soothing touch of those thin fingers of his. "She said she put in only a very little of the arsenic compound for Mark to get—it was another step in

202

her fear campaign against him—but, of course, you got it instead. And then, when you staggered into Mrs. Thursten's bedroom, Carol was in there, trying on her Sybil disguise ahead of time for the séance. You were lying on the floor, and when she bent over you she realized at once you were very ill. She didn't know what to do—you needed immediate help, but she didn't want to be caught in her Sybil getup. So she made a lot of noise, enough to be sure that Mark would hear it and come to Sybil's room; then she ran back to her own room." Dion looked at me. "What happened to you really shook the rest of us. Especially me. I was growing fond of my fair enchantress."

I laughed shakily. "Is that how you all thought of me? Anyway, if Mark killed his wife at four o'clock, according to Bobbie, who heard but didn't see it, how could he have been with me at four? I remember distinctly it was four."

He left me and circled the room, thinking this over. Turning from the window, he asked, "How do you know it was four? Your testimony said the desk clock. And what else?"

"My watch, of course! No. Wait. Mark brought me a charm bracelet for my birthday. He took off my watch to put on the bracelet." I gasped at the insistence I had shown on the witness stand. "I believe I said I looked at my watch. But I couldn't have. Mark had it in his hand. I only looked at the desk clock."

Dion's eyes lighted. "And he could easily have set the desk clock back an hour. That must be the answer."

It was strange to realize that all the mysterious doings, the attempts to frighten Mark and me, even Mrs. Jeffrey's conduct the first night—and it must have been she who had played Sybil outside the lanai window, wearing a blonde wig and heavy make-up—had been a plot to force a confession from us. I understood now, too, the activity both in the attic and in Mrs. Thursten's bedroom—those were the places where her clothes, needed for the Sybil appearances, were kept. "I saw Carol on the attic stairs yesterday," I said suddenly. "She must have been testing her resemblance to her sister. She was dressed like Mrs. Thursten. I nearly fainted."

"Thank God we were wrong about you. I wish I had never gotten involved with the Jeffreys' revenge plan. But when I heard of Mrs. Thursten's death, and her killer about to go free, I kept remembering how good she had been to all of us in the ward. Between us, the Jeffrey women and I convinced ourselves we had the right to put a scare into you two."

"What about Mark's locked study, and his messed-up desk?" I asked. "And I found a flashlight battery in there—was that from that little round electronic light you were carrying tonight? Did you or Mrs. Jeffrey do that to the study, as a part of the fear plan?"

"Yes," Dion said. "That was part of the keep-Thursten-worrying strategy, too."

I suddenly remembered my first night at Beach House when I had thought the shine of the flashlight in Dion's hand was from a knife or a gun. Had that only been the other night? It seemed like an eon ago. I brought my thoughts back to the present.

"The one we should really pity is Bobbie," I said soberly, depressed by the thought. "She was almost ready to forget her suspicions of her father."

He took my hand in his, looked at me with that dark-eyed gaze I had first noticed, and then, advising me to get some rest, he left me.

Early in the morning I did sleep a little. Then I was awakened by the sound of an unfamiliar motor warming up. I scrambled out of bed and rushed to the window in time to see Bobbie and Mark getting into the back seat of a police car. They had their arms around each other. Strange, and terribly poignant to me, that the actual arrest of her father should bring Bobbie to this mature and compassionate state. Perhaps she even understood the violence in his nature which, at two crises, had burst out in murder.

I felt my own cowardice, but the truth is, I was relieved that I need not see the two of them again in Beach House, where there had been so much horror. I packed my things and was ready when Dion came for me. He brought a brief message of regret from Mrs. Jeffrey, who seemed understandably glad that the murderer of her two daughters had been apprehended at least, though she was in a terrible state of grief.

"She knows now that you weren't involved," Dion explained. I felt sorry for her. But I was sorriest for Bobbie, and proud of her too.

When I left the Beach House, I left it forever, with the man whom I had finally learned to trust.

"And I love that loyalty in you, Livy. That loyalty and devotion to Thursten. All the lovely things that make you the girl I—" He grinned. "Isn't it lucky that besides all those admirable qualities, you're pretty too?"

I felt infinitely better. Dion Bates, I found, could always make me feel better.